UMBILICAL

OLIVER'S STORY

VOLUME 1

By

Gordon Richardson

MAPLE
PUBLISHERS

UMBILICAL OLIVER'S STORY – VOLUME 1

Author: Gordon Richardson

Copyright © 2025 Gordon Richardson

The right of Gordon Richardson to be identified as author of this work has been asserted by the author in accordance with section 77 and 78 of the Copyright, Designs and Patents Act 1988.

First Published in 2025

ISBN 978-1-83538-473-2 (Paperback)
978-1-83538-474-9 (Hardback)
978-1-83538-475-6 (E-Book)

Book Cover Design and Book Layout by:
White Magic Studios
www.whitemagicstudios.co.uk

Published by:
Maple Publishers
Fairbourne Drive, Atterbury,
Milton Keynes,
MK10 9RG, UK
www.maplepublishers.com

A CIP catalogue record for this title is available from the British Library.

CONTENTS

Here I am again in this relentless nightmare, which I cannot stop or control, I have tried many times without success. It started about a year ago, it would happen at about every two to three week intervals, I am now having them every few days or so, mom says she knows when I am having these nightmares, she can hear me from her bedroom across the hall and says it's a quite frightening to hear me, but she cannot do anything only comfort me, she says I make a sound like a muffled scream, then when I do awake, it's as if the scream is released, and I wake up shouting and screaming at the top of my voice,

I am wringing wet with sweat, that is when mom comes to my rescue with clean dry pyjamas and sheets.

I tell my mom I am so sorry, over and over again, but she said it does not matter. The doctor says it is only a temporary thing, and you will eventually grow out of the dreams. I feel very guilty and sorry for my mom, as she has to get up early tomorrow, she works in a cafe, and is on her feet all day, she is up early to bake apple pies and cupcakes for the cafe, to earn extra money, it's not good for my mom, but what makes life harder, is I do not have a dad. Mom says he left just after my third birthday she says "one day he will come back" well it's my fourteenth birthday tomorrow so I have serious doubts that he will, but I would never say that to mom, I have no photographs of him, according to mom, all my grandparents died before I was born, both my grandad's were killed in the second world war, moms dad who was a merchant seaman died when the ship he was on was torpedoed by a German u boat, and all hands were lost, my other grandad was reported missing in action, one of my nan's died from cancer, mom says the other nan, she believes died from a broken heart from never knowing what happened to her beloved husband. Mom asked me about my dream again, hoping I think that talking about it may resolve why this is happening to me, up to yet no luck.

My nightmare

It always starts the same, where I'm looking down at my bare feet, I'm standing on grass I can see it poking through between my toes, I look up, and there is a full moon, my instincts tell me to look behind me, and I get a shock as I realise I am standing a matter of inches away from a sheer drop, in other words a cliff edge, which made me jump forward, but curiosity got the better of me I had to look over the edge, and I could see a river far below, with large areas of dense pine forests.

I moved away from the cliff edge and turned around, I realise, I am looking down a grassy slope, and at the bottom of the slope there is a stream, I can see and hear the water trickling over the rocks, on the other side of the stream is almost a mirror image of the slope I am now standing on. Looking to my left is a cliff face, rising high above me, stark white in the moonlight, the only thing breaking this whiteness, are a few small trees that have managed to find a home in the cracks and crevices, as my eyes wander across the cliff face.

I realise I am looking at the streams source, a beautiful waterfall cascading down from the top of the cliff, my eyes follow the waterfall down to where it crashes onto the rocks below, creating this white mist, I can feel the moisture in the air on my face as a gentle breeze brings this ghostly mist towards me, sometimes enveloping me, then clearing as the breeze changes course, to my right is a dense dark forest of pine trees, which end just before the stream, and then continues on up the opposite hill,, my gaze returned to the white cliff face, I noticed it carried on past the waterfall to the top of the opposite hill, before disappearing into the distance. This white cliff must carry on for miles.

There was a full moon, the sky was very clear, not a cloud anywhere, the other thing which was quite noticeable, over the brow of the opposite hill and beyond it, a bright white light, changing to an orange glow then fading to blue then back to white, I thought I know what that is, there is a fast food restaurant over that hill and that is the lights from their advertising signs, which gave me a bit of comfort knowing there maybe people over the hill. I am standing next to a cliff edge, in a strange place, bare feet, and in my pyjamas. To one side of me is a rock face, the other side, a dark forest. I hear things scurrying around in the forest, I can hear cracking and rustling sounds which could be an animal, or something, maybe someone had trodden on a branch or branches in the forest, which then prompted me to move farther away from there fast.

As I made my way down the hill, I suddenly let out this yelp as I had stubbed my toe on something in the grass, which turned out to be lumps of rock, there was a lot more as I approached the stream and waterfall, so I had to be careful where I trod, on reaching the edge of the stream to my left I could see the waterfall, which was occasionally obscured by the spray and mist, this huge white curtain of water falling maybe a hundred ft.. from the cliff top, It was quite beautiful.

Looking at the base of the waterfall every so often the mist and spray would clear, and I noticed a dark almost circular shape at the back of the waterfall, Instantly I thought wow, a cave, I wondered if this was where I had to go, I am obviously meant to go somewhere, perhaps this is it, so I slowly moved forward getting very wet, I went to the edge of the waterfall and tried to get behind the curtain of water, which was very difficult, but I made it but was very disappointed finding the cave to be only three or four ft.. deep, going nowhere. I left the cave on the opposite side of the waterfall, absolutely drenched and cold.

As I stood there shivering water dripping off me, I looked down at the stream and my eyes followed its path, as it wound its way over and between the rocks of this long stream, eventually disappearing altogether to the valley below. The valley was beautiful in the moonlight. I could see this ribbon of water deep down in the valley. In the distance I could see snow-capped mountains, and the stars twinkling in the dark sky above. Then I heard a noise which brought me back down to earth with a bump. I had difficulty in recognising the sound, because of the noise from the waterfall, or even the direction of the sound.

I then decided my best option is to head up this grassy slope towards those lights, hoping that there may be civilization on the other side, perhaps somebody can help me get back to my home and my mom. Maybe tell me where I am, how, did I get here and why am I here? So, I started up the hill, slipping quite a few times on the wet grass and my wet feet, eventually getting to drier grass, where I could walk normally. I had only taken about another ten or so steps, when I realised I was not alone.

Looking up I saw the figure of a man on the brow of the hill. The light or lights behind him were so bright I had to raise my hands in front of me to shield my eyes from the brightness. I tried to make out the man's features, but it was impossible because of the intense light behind him. I knew he was quite tall, and I knew he had long hair, because I could see it blowing about in the breeze. I called out to him, "Can you help me please?" He did not say anything, but put his hands out towards me, then it hit me Oh god I'm dead, and this is Jesus welcoming me into heaven, this cannot be! I don't remember dying. With this crazy thought racing through my mind, I thought what am I going to do? Then it struck me, this must be a dream, I will wake up soon.

But then why does everything feel and look so real? The grass under my feet feels real, my stubbed toe is still throbbing, the water and the cold feel real enough. I thought, right if he is my saviour, I am going to him. I looked to the figure on the hill, but I realised he is no longer holding his arms out towards me, but his arms are now at his side, it appears he is now looking to his left towards the forest. He seems to be listening and looking for something, he then becomes quite agitated, looking at me then looking into the distance.

He looked down at me, and shouted to me which sounded like 'go go'. But with the strong light behind him, I could not tell whether he was gesturing for me to go towards him or to run away from him. Puzzled, I just stood still, then I felt it. The ground shook, and a few seconds later a loud cracking sound, a sound like trees being snapped, then falling to the ground - whatever this was, it was coming my way, there was a huge thudding sound, I then realised something very big was walking towards me.

Obviously trees are not an obstacle to whatever it was that was approaching me. Above the clamour of the trees falling I could hear a loud grunting and snorting, which made the hairs on the back of my neck stand up. I looked once more at the man on the hill, and still could not understand which way he wanted me to go. Do I go up the hill towards him? I then thought better of the devil you know, so I decided to run as fast as I could the way I came. I had no choice, it was either to be crushed or snapped like the trees, or leap off the cliff into oblivion, hoping to miss the rocks below and into the river.

So I started to run but could not get a grip. I started to slip on the wet grass, I then realised I was not going to make it across the stream and over the other side and up the slope. My only refuge was the cave at the back of the waterfall, so I headed for it, slipping and sliding. Eventually I got to the stream, I could hear the last few trees going down which prompted me to run faster up the stream, which was only a short distance, but seemed to take forever. I eventually reached the waterfall and ran through it to the cave behind.

I then crouched down in the cave, hoping to be as least visible as possible, hoping the swirling mist and the waterfall will hide me and the cave from whatever I presumed was chasing me. The sound of the trees breaking and falling had stopped, but I could still hear that thudding sound, the ground was shaking more violently now, so much so that pieces of rock were falling off the cave wall. I knew this thing was heading towards the waterfall and me, I suddenly realised the night had become much darker.

This thing, this creature, was blocking most of the only light there was, which was the moonlight, so how big is it? I also noticed the ground had stopped shaking, so I knew it was standing there looking for me. But why me? Has this got something to do with the strange man on the hill, perhaps it is looking for him and not me? There is no way I am going out there and asking who the hell it is looking for, so I thought I've got to find a way out of here. I had noticed an outcrop of rock, just above the cave, which split part of the waterfall, which gave an intermittent clear view to the outside. I then got myself into a position so I could see through the gap in the waterfall, hoping to see whatever was out there. I strained my eyes to see in the poor light.

When I saw it, I recoiled in absolute horror. This thing was so big, I could not see its upper body and head from where I was positioned, but what I could see terrified me. The first thing I noticed was how long its arms were, its hands, if you could call them hands, actually touched the floor, then it moved, and I could see the so-called hands more clearly. It had two large claws, on each hand with very pointed tips instead of a thumb, it had a single much bigger and very sharp looking claw, so if this thing gripped you there would be no escape. It seemed to be covered in some kind of brown scruffy fur, is this a Bigfoot or a yeti? I have read about and seen programmes on telly about these creatures, but they never looked anything like this.

It started to turn slightly, then I caught sight of its legs and lower body, its legs and feet were massive, its feet appeared to be huge and round they reminded me of elephants feet, and had one huge claw at the front of each foot, as this thing lifted its foot to turn to look around, I had a clear view of the claw, which was huge and curved, ending in a sharp point, which reminded me of an eagle's beak. I really needed to see what this thing's head looked like, so I decided, perhaps if I lay on my back, and tilted my head as far back as I could, I might be able to get a glimpse of its head. Sure enough it worked and what I saw terrified me. Its head was huge and round, it had no ears as I could see, but boy! Did it have eyes and a mouth - a mouth which was not really a mouth? What would have been its top lip, was a huge sharp curved beak, its bottom beak slightly smaller, its beak mouth opening and closing all the time, letting out these deep grunting sounds.

What the hell is it? A bear, a bird and an elephant. Its eyes were an even more weird feature - it had two eyes alright, but not in the configuration that we are used to. All creatures I can think of including humans have them opposite each other - one on the left one on the right. This thing had two huge eyes, one above the other its forehead was huge, the upper eye was a deep red, larger than the lower one, and in the centre of the red was this pulsing bright green orb, that expanded and contracted, at times almost covering the red. The lower eye was of the most beautiful blue I have ever seen. It shimmered like a blue pool of water. There did not seem to be any eyelids, I never once saw it blink all the time I watched it. I then got back into a kneeling position, and moved round to the gap in the waterfall so I could see what he was up to. While I was watching him, I was shocked when this small figure suddenly emerged from behind the creature. This really took me by surprise, I rubbed my eyes, but no, this figure was still there.

I realised it was this tiny man, about five feet tall he was wearing what appeared to be this red and gold costume. It was only when he came closer I realised he was wearing traditional Chinese clothing. It had golden dragons beautifully embroidered on those droopy sleeves they have, these golden dragons were also across his chest and around the bottom edges of what I presumed to be a coat. He had quite a large round face, and I could just make out his thin black droopy moustache. I remember from pictures I have seen, they wear a small black hat.

This man definitely did not, as I could quite plainly see the moonlight reflecting off his bald shiny head, much like a Billiard ball. One of the most distinctive things about him was the staff he was holding in his right hand. It was taller than him by about a foot. At the top of the staff was what looked like a golden open hand, its fingers and thumb pointing upwards, and in the hand was what appeared to be a bird, black and shiny, perhaps a raven or something. It was only when he turned to the huge creature that I really saw what it was. It was not a bird, but a small black dragon, with bright red eyes.

Perhaps the tiny dragon was carved from ebony, or some sort of black rock. As far as I could see it was beautifully carved, the Chinese and Japanese are very good at doing these intricate carvings. But then, while I was looking at it, I could swear I saw it move, I must be mistaken, perhaps the mist swirling about gave me the impression that it had moved, I could not take my eyes off it. Then I saw it, there was no doubt this time, I clearly saw it turn its head and look up into the moonlit sky then turn its head back and stare directly in my direction; sheer panic, my stomach turned over, could it see me.

It was still staring. I held my breath, then a huge sigh of relief, when I saw it turn its head away from me, it obviously hadn't seen me thank God, I then heard shouting, I realised it was the little Chinese man, and was shouting at the creature, I could not make out everything he was saying, but was obviously very angry. I heard him speaking in English, but with a strong Chinese accent. The words I clearly heard were - "You stupid fool, I clear trees for you, and you still let him escape." That shook me, the giant didn't clear a path through the trees, the little Chinese man was saying that he did it, how can that be?

Perhaps I need to be more afraid of the little man than the giant. This huge creature was obviously terrified of him; so this little Chinese man must have tremendous powers, or has a hold of some sort over the creature, this monster could quite easily destroy him if he wanted to. The Chinese man had now stopped shouting, the creature was quiet and still, probably too frightened to make a move or a sound. My eyes were fixed on the little man waiting to see what he was going to do next.

I did not have to wait long. I saw him raise his staff a few inches off the ground, then bring it back down, with considerable force, making the tiny dragon screech and flap its wings in protest. The Chinaman looked up at the dragon, and in a stern voice, just uttered one word, "find". The dragon instantly flew off, circling overhead a few times, before flying off into the distance. I then suddenly realised that this little man, and his creature, who were hunting me down, for no reason I can think of, used the tiny dragon to find me. I remember when I stubbed my toe on a rock, coming down the slope, I heard a noise

Above me, looking up I saw what I took to be a small bat. It seemed to circle above me for a few seconds, before flying off. I thought it must have been a bat, because of that leathery flapping sound its wings made, and I did not think any more of it, but now it made sense, that's why they were able to come straight to me, his little spy in the sky made sure of that. After a few minutes the dragon came back, circled overhead a few times, then landed back on its perch, its claws gripping the upturned fingers of the golden hand on top of the Chinaman's staff, with its head up and with its wings outstretched, which must be a sign to its master, that it can't find me, which made the Chinaman even angrier, banging his staff hard on the ground, making the dragon lose its balance. It then flew off, probably finding somewhere safe, till its master's temper cooled down. It was then I saw the little man turn, and look towards where I had seen the man that looked like Jesus on the brow of the hill. He seemed to tilt his head to one side, as if listening to something. I heard a voice, coming from the direction of where the Chinaman was looking, I moved to the edge of the waterfall, and looked up the hill.

I could see what the Chinaman was looking at, it was that strange man, standing on top of the hill again. He had seemed to disappear at the same time that I ran behind the waterfall. He was waving his hands and arms about and shouting, I heard him say, "Over here, he's over here," and I realised he was creating a diversion for me. I heard the little Chinaman shout at the creature, "Get him." I heard a roar, and the ground started to shake again. I guessed the creature was on the move, heading towards the top of the hill, where that strange man was standing. I saw the shadow of this huge creature pass the waterfall, appearing to cross the stream in one giant stride.

I knew it would not take long for the monster and the little man to get to the top of the hill, that giant claw on the front of the creature's foot would give it tremendous grip, so if I was going to do something, I had better do it now, and fast. I needed to run towards that cliff edge where this terrible nightmare had started. I then ran through the edge of the waterfall, the water blinded me for a few seconds, but luckily, I had landed on the grass bank on the edge of the stream, but my heart sank, when I found myself slipping backwards into the stream.

Sheer panic set in, I looked to my left, and noticed the bank was lower, a few feet away. I scrambled over to it, and noticed there were rocks embedded in the bank, which I managed to grab, and was able to pull myself out of the stream. Already out of breath, I started to run, but slipped again, and fell on my hands and knees. I thought, my god, I am not going to make it. Just when I thought things couldn't get any worse, I heard the words that absolutely terrified me: "There he is, get him."

The Chinaman had obviously spotted me. Taking a deep breath, I managed to get to my feet. Still slipping on the wet grass I managed to gain a couple of yards, then I remembered the rocks I had stubbed my toe on earlier, so moving to my right, I found them, which gave me the grip I needed, I had not noticed before but there were lots of the little white chunks of rock, which must have broken off at some time in the past, all along the edge of the cliff face, that towered above me, so keeping close to the cliff face, I started to run picking up speed. The stones were hurting my bare feet, but I did not care, because I could feel and hear that creature gaining on me. But what do I do when I get to the cliff edge? The only hope I have is to dive into the river below, that I had seen when I had looked over the cliff edge earlier. I can only hope and pray that I can make it.

Absolutely exhausted, I managed to make it to the cliff edge, and I knew I would not be able to hesitate, else that thing would have me, so with my hands together in a diving position, I dove off the edge. As I did, I heard this loud snap. Just behind me the creature had tried to grab me, but missed. That was the sound of its claws snapping shut, I was now in space, hurtling towards what I hope is the river below,

But to my absolute horror, I realised I was not going to dive into the river, but onto the rocks that formed the river bank, which in the moonlight the white sharp rocks, seem to resemble teeth. That's when I started to scream, but just before I was about to hit the rocks, I woke up, screaming. Someone had once told me that if you ever do reach the bottom of your fall, you die in your dream and in real life.

Enlightenment

Woke up this morning feeling great, bright eyed and bushy tailed as mom would say. Mom said it looks like you have had a good restful night's sleep. That may be due to the fact, I haven't had one of those horrible nightmares for over two weeks now. I am going to get ready for school, as I have to help mom carry the boxes of apple pies and cakes to the cafe on the high street before going to school. Since those horrible dreams have stopped, I am feeling much better, I still can't figure it out. Those dreams just didn't make any sense.

A strange thing I had to wake mom the other night, as I thought I had heard someone or something in my wardrobe, the noises were only faint. It's only when I heard my coat hangers rattling together, that made me really scared, but as usual, no nonsense mom, strides over to the wardrobe, swings the doors open in one swift move, and puts her head in and shouts, "Anybody in there?" Silence as we both listened, then mom swung my clothes backwards and forwards, my coat hangers making a screeching noise as they slid over the metal rail that my clothes were hanging on, putting my nerves even more on edge.

She turned round to me smiling, and said, "Look no bogeyman," as she pulled the clothes back, so that I could see right to the back of the wardrobe. I said, "Ok mom, but I am sure I heard something in there, and I know I heard the coat hangers rattle together." Mom said, "Look, try and get to sleep, perhaps it was the wind." I looked at mom, and said, "Come on mom, wind in my wardrobe? You will be saying there's rain in the attic next." Standing in the doorway, she turned to me, with that lovely warm smile she has, and said, "Actually we have clever clogs," and in a stern voice, she said, "Get to sleep."

Well, I am ready to go to school, just waiting for mom to finish putting the apple pies and cakes into the boxes we use to carry them to the café. Mom finished putting the lids on the boxes and picked one of them up, she said, "Are you ready Oliver?" By the way, that's my name, Olly to my friends, but mom does not like them calling me Olly, she says, "You were named Oliver they should call you that." Anyway I may as well describe myself. I am average height for my age, mom says I am a bit skinny, but will fill out as I get older.

I have almost white blond hair, mom says she believes my hair colour was called flaxen hair by the ancient Britons. Mom calls me her pretty boy, which I don't particularly like. It's because I like my hair quite long, she said because of my long hair, big blue eyes and small features, from a distance, I look more like a girl, but I don't care, I like me as I am, although that may be the reason I get bullied a lot, and even if I had my hair cut, I think | would still be bullied. Mom's friends and the teachers at school all say how polite and quiet I am, but that is how mom has taught me.

The next day mom was baking. She said to me Oliver, you know in life you will get much farther with a spoon of honey, than you will with a spoon of vinegar, in other words be kind and respectful to people and it will be returned. "But mom," I said, "that does not always work, some people do not appreciate kindness and respect." Well mom was kneading dough at the time, she had flour all over her hands, on her face, and even in her hair, she very quickly turned around to me, with an angry look I had never seen before, with fists clenched her eyes flashing with anger, her lips drawn back over her teeth, she spat the words out at me, "Well give them a damn spoon of vinegar then." She saw the look on my face, she realised how much she had frightened me.

With her arms reaching out towards me, and with tears in her eyes, she said, "Oliver, I am so sorry." But by then I had backed away from her. Realising she may frighten me even more, she turned back to her baking. I then moved towards my mom, as I had realised from the shaking of her shoulders, and her tears dropping into the flour on the worktop, creating little moon like crater circles in the flour, seeing my mom so sad, started me crying as well, so I ran up to her, and put my arms around her. You see, I know she worries about me being bullied at school. Not having my father here must put a great strain on her, she must be missing him, but mom is a very strong person and does not give up if she believes in something, so she will never give up on my dad.

On at least two occasions, she has been to see the headmaster, and what I can gather, gave him a real good tongue lashing. The headmaster in his defence, has stopped quite a lot of the bullying, but it is impossible to stop all of it, as a lot of it happens on the way home, and of course anytime, and anywhere, when we are out playing. It is an impossibility for teachers or parents to follow and protect us 24 hours a day.

I have learned to cope with the name calling, and the physical abuse, the punches in the guts, ribs back of the head, slaps in the face, tripping you up especially when your arms are full of books, and of course the classic head down the toilet routine, where they hold your head down the toilet then flush it. It's not too bad most times you just get your hair wet, but it's not so good when they put your head in the toilet, after stinky meldrew has been in there. We do not know what he eats, but the smell is terrible. I did hear about one of the smaller boys they did it to, where they put his head in the toilet where smelly had done a, no two and had not flushed. Ugh! My best friend Rueben gets bullied more than I do. Rueben's quite small, he told me he comes from a Jewish family.

He has dark hair and his eyes are almost black, he wears those silly big glasses, making his eyes look huge. He wears short trousers, which do not help, as he has some of the skinniest legs I have ever seen. To top it all, he has big feet, so it looks like he has two matchsticks sticking out of his trousers with boots on, and of course he was given the nickname of Milly, as his surname is Millhouse; he may as well have put a sign round his neck saying, come and beat me up.

But I know Rueben has a good soul, he is kind and thoughtful. He often gives me little gifts for my mom. He had seen mom in town one day and it had started to rain. Luckily mom had her mac on, but had forgotten her brolly. Next day at school Milly gave me a little package, and said, "That's for your mom." "Thanks Mill," I said, "that's very kind of you Mill." He then puts his hands in his pockets and stares at the floor, drawing an imaginary circle with his foot, and without looking up, he said, "It's ok." When I got home, mom was out in the garden. I called out to her, "Rueben's sent you a present." She looked up.

With a puzzled look on her face, she got up from where she was weeding and started to walk towards me, as she did so, taking her garden gloves off still looking puzzled, she came into the kitchen. "Well," she said, "Where is it?" I said, "Over there on the table." She walked over and picked it up. Holding the parcel, she turned her head, screwing her eyes up at me. Smiling, she said, "Is this one of your silly jokes, nothing is going to jump out at me is there?" "No, honestly mom, Rueben said it's a present for you." "Ok god help you, if it's one of those joke things."

She started to unwrap it, she held it up. It was about six inches long and about two inches square made of soft plastic. I could see it had a little fold over flap, with one of those little press studs to keep it shut. The colour of it was like a sky blue, with pretty flowers along the edge of it. Mom snapped open the flap, and pulled out what was inside. We both looked at it, it was one of those plastic rain hats. Mom opened it out, it was a soft clear plastic decorated with pretty flowers.

Mom put it on her head and tied the two strings under her chin, she looked down at the wrapper and realised he had written on it, "To Olly's mom, saw you in the town. Your hair got wet, sorry, couldn't afford an umbrella, hope this will help, Rueben." Mom pulled out a chair and sat down. I looked into her face, I could see tears welling up in her eyes, then a tear rolled down her cheek, with a quiver in her voice, she said, "This is your best friend that little Jewish boy, that you said was bullied terrible at school, and yet he still finds the kindness in his heart, to be good to other people." With tears running down both cheeks now, and tears in my own eyes mom said very quietly, "Bless him."

Both of us are still being bullied, in and out of school, but I have learned not to let mom know about it, as I have seen how upset she gets. The one we dare not tell her about, is where we have to walk down an alleyway to get to and back from school. The alley is about fifteen ft.. wide, and is quite long but it looks narrow because people put their bins along their garden walls, which back onto the alley. Some have decided to put their bins on the opposite wall, which makes it harder and narrower for us to get through without being beaten up, or our lunch money taken from us, most times our lunch as well.

So when we come from school, we look down the alley, to see if the three big boy bullies are waiting for us. If we can't see them, sometimes we will run the gauntlet, and weave between the bins as fast as we can, sometimes we make it, and sometimes we don't. They hide behind the bins, and jump out on us, pinning us to the ground, sitting on us, until we give them what they want. When they eventually let us up, they always give us a kick in the pants, or a smack round the ear, or both. Not satisfied with sitting on us, till we cannot breathe, and stealing from us, they have to hit us as well.

The reason we risk going down the alley is the road to the right of the alley swings round in a wide arc, but it is a long way round, sometimes we have to go that way, then mom starts to worry when we are late coming home. To the left of the alley, mom says is a no go area, as the street we have to turn down is a bad area and is known for drug dealing, and drug addicts roaming the street. The police are there nearly all the time, so we never go that way. You see, mom thinks we always come to and from school through the alleyway.

Mom knows about these boys, who hang about in the alleyway. One day walking down the alley, I decided I had enough of these thugs. Mom had given me some money, to go to the tuck shop, to get some sweets for me and Mill. She also gave me extra money to get her favourite bar of chocolate, which was a treat for her and come hell or high water, that's what I was going to get for her, so when these two boys stepped out and blocked our way, I stood my ground and Mill stood behind me. I heard him whisper to me in a rather shaky voice, "I'm watching your back." "Oh yes Milly, you're watching my back, who's watching yours?" I should never have doubted him.

I swear I could hear Mill's knees knocking together, which really did not inspire me with much confidence, nevertheless I intended to complete my mission. The more aggressive of the two bullies stood in front of me. This was Jake, one of the most evil looking persons you will ever meet. He had mousey coloured curly hair, strangely his hair had a greenish hue, which quite perfectly matched his teeth. I don't think he knows what a toothbrush is, his teeth were a dark colour, with bits of black decay between them. He always had this sickly grin on his face, so when he confronts you, that's the first thing you see, those horrible teeth, and the white spittle that seems to collect in the corners of that horrible cruel mouth of his. He has spots on his chin, and around his mouth, a lot of them are red with yellow pus in them. The most noticeable was the large one on the end of his nose. It was very red, with a bright yellow top to it, which reminded me of a volcano ready to explode, but it is the eyes that are the most frightening.

Like most things about him they are green, a dark green, they have a look of savage cruelty in them that I have never seen in anybody's eyes before. When he is threatening you, he looks deep into your eyes, I believe he is maybe trying to steal my soul. For I am sure he is the devil incarnate. If the devil has possessed him, he has picked the right person, because Jake is fairly tall, is quite muscular, and is fast on his feet and has this evil aura about him. There is no escaping him. So I am going to try and avoid that withering stare of his, as usually I am like a rabbit caught in a car's headlights. Freezing on the spot, too frightened to move till it's too late. I am usually that rabbit, but not today. So I swallowed hard, or I tried to swallow because suddenly my mouth had become very dry, even when my tongue temporarily stuck to the roof of my mouth. I was still determined, I was not going to be bullied by these people anymore; so I confronted him.

I had already decided whatever happens, I must not look into those eyes or I am lost, I looked him squarely in the nose, which was fatal, because as soon as I saw that big red spot with all the yellow in it, I had the urge to squeeze it, which made me think, 'here is this tough guy, with something almost akin to a clown's nose,' and putting my hand over my mouth, I started to laugh well, giggle really, big mistake. I saw him look across to his brother who was standing about ten feet away, smoking a cigarette.

He usually did not bother us too much, he would kick us in the pants, as we walked or ran by. He would laugh when his cruel brother hurt and frightened us. His gaze then went to his dad, who was leaning against his garden wall, a pig of a man, he was dirty, looked like he had never had a wash in his life. He was a big man, about six ft. tall, he wore these grey trousers which had turn ups around the leg bottoms. They were covered in stains and dirt, the stains were more than likely beer, and god knows what else. The vest that he always seemed to be wearing looked more stained and dirtier than the trousers. The only good thing about the vest was that it covered the huge gut that was hanging over the top of those trousers. His hair was quite long, untidy and receding at the front he looked as if he had not shaved for days.

A cigarette hung from the corner of his mouth, the ash on the cigarette was well over an inch long, and was defying gravity very well, until he coughed, and the ash drifted off into the wind. He had the usual can of beer in his hand. All around his slippered feet were at least half a dozen crushed beer cans. I could tell he was drunk, because his eyes were red rimmed with that glazed look, he was also having trouble standing. Jake then shouted to his father, "Dad he's laughing at me." His dad slowly lifted his head, and said, "Well don't just stand there, smash his face in." I ignored his father, and determined to have my say, I stopped laughing, and became serious, and I said, "Look Jake, you are a bully."

My Saviour

I do not remember much else, only what appeared to be a bright orange flash of light and a sound in my head, which sounded like "dong", as if somebody had struck a very large bell, with a very big hammer, but little did I realise, that the hammer was Jake's fist, and the bell was my nose and forehead. Luckily, most of the force of the punch was on my forehead, if it hadn't, I would surely be nursing a broken nose.

The next thing that I remember, I could feel this jolting and shaking all through my body, and I realised I was being carried by someone, and as I looked up through blurry eyes, I recognised it was Mr O'Conner that was carrying me. Mr O'Conner lived in the house on the corner, not far from the alleyway, he must have obviously come to our rescue, I saw him look down at me, and say, Hi Olly, welcome back to the living as he had realised I had come round. He said, "Don't worry, I am just taking you and your friend back to my house. we will get you cleaned up before you go home."

I loved to hear Mr. O'Conner talk, as he spoke with a soft Irish brogue that was quite comforting. He put me down just in front of his open front door. "You ok to walk Oliver?" "Yes thank you, Mr. O'Conner, I'll be alright." Then it dawned on me. "Milly," I said, "Where is my friend Milly, is he ok?" Before Mr. O'Conner could answer, I heard Milly shout "I'm here I'm ok." I said, "Thank god for that, I thought Jake had got you and hurt you as well." "In a way he did." "Tell me what happened?" Before Milly could answer, Mr. O'Conner spoke. "I'll tell you what happened, your friend there is a diamond, a very brave little friend you have there." Mr O'Conner said, "Because it has been hot today, I had my front door and side window open, I was just sitting there reading my newspaper, when I heard Jake's voice. Guessing he was up to no good, as usual, I decided to have a look at what was going on, so I looked down into the alley way, and I saw your friend standing about ten feet behind Jake. I saw you standing in front of him, Jake's brother was to your right, and their disgusting father was leaning against the wall."

"I then looked back to you, and realised you were laughing or chuckling to yourself. I realised by the look on Jake's face, he was not a happy bunny, I started to walk forward. I had only taken a few steps, when I heard him shout to his father, I thought to myself-is this kid crazy? He's laughing at the most obnoxious and violent families in the area I knew he was going to hit you. I started to run, and shouted at him to leave you alone, but before I had even finished my sentence, he had hit you full in the face, you went crashing to the ground."

"Jake's brother and father panicked when they saw me coming towards them, the father got to the six foot wooden garden gate first, but in his drunken stupor couldn't find the handle to open the gate, the son in his panic, crashed into the back of his father, both shouting and swearing at each other, managing to open the gate, they both fell into a heap on their garden pathway, with the father swearing at his son, telling him to lock the gate. I tried to ignore them as best as I could, I was more focused on you lying on the ground, and what Jake was going to do next."

"But it looked as if Jake was going to stand his ground, unlike the rest of his family, he had stayed exactly where he was. I continued to walk steadily towards him when I was about ten feet away from you, lying there. I could see blood on your face and shirt, you weren't moving at all. Seeing you there made me very angry. Then something very unexpected happened, there was this loud scream which stopped me in my tracks, I saw this tiny figure leap onto Jake's back. One arm was locked around Jake's neck, the other little arm had a fist on the end of it which was pummelling the side of Jake's face. I realised Oliver, it was your friend. Milly, I think you call him, he was screaming in Jake's ear, 'you've killed my friend' over and over again, that was until Jake picked him off his back and held him at arm's length, looked at him for a second as if he was some irritating bug, then threw him at me with considerable force, knocking me backwards. I managed to hold on to your friend."

"But it had made me stumble backwards, nearly falling over you, but by the time I had put your friend down, Jake had disappeared. So then I made sure your friend Milly was ok. I picked you up and carried you back here." "Thank you, Mr O'Conner, but why are they so frightened of you?" "Well my dad used to be a boxer, and from an early age, taught me how to box. When I was about 16 years old I did some amateur boxing. I really enjoyed it, as I won all of my first matches. But let's get inside first, and if you are still interested I will tell you.

"We entered Mr' O'Conner's house and there was this lovely smell of cheese on toast, one of the nicest smells on earth. Mr O'Connor said do you boys want something to eat, no thank you, Mr' O'Connor, Ok then, you boys sit down, we sat down on this very springy two-seater settee. Look you boys please call me Shamus I prefer it, Ok. Yes Mr, I mean Shamus. Mill piped up please carry on telling us about your boxing. Ok where was I, oh yes. I won most of my fights in the first or second round. My dad, who was my trainer, and my mentor taught me so much, not just about boxing, but about life and to trust my instincts and my gut feelings, and he was right, bless his cotton socks." Which made me and Milly laugh, then I asked him, thinking of how my mom would react if I suddenly took up boxing, "Did your mom mind you doing it?" "Well she did not like it at the start, and tried to stop me from going into what she said was a very dangerous sport, it caused a few problems between mom and dad.

But relented later, as she could see I was determined to do this. Mom did win in the end though. I was doing really well, the first five fights I won by knockout, in the sixth fight, I won on points and I only just beat him. I then realised my next fights were going to get a lot tougher, which proved to be the case in my seventh fight, when I got into the ring, I looked over at my opponent, he did not look anything special, he was a bit taller than me, but my instincts told me there was more to this guy, he did not' seem to be in the least bit nervous.

He just stared at me, never taking his eyes off me, till the ref called us to the centre of the ring. Milly suddenly said, "Did you beat him?" Yeah I beat him alright by the skin of my teeth, he beat the crap out of me, he knocked me down twice, I just about beat him on points. When I got home, mom just took one look at me, and burst into tears. She looked at my dad, and said, 'This is your fault. Just look at the state of him." She was right, I was in a bit of a mess.

My left eye was completely closed, I had a gash over my right eye where he had head butted me. Dad had to take me to hospital to get it stitched up, I had to have my bottom lip stitched as well, the left side of my face was badly swollen, it hurt to breathe where he had pummelled my ribs. Mom was so angry, she said to my dad, 'Look at what you have done to my baby with your stupid boxing, I can hardly recognise him.' She walked up to my dad, with one hand on her hip, and the forefinger of her other hand waving menacingly in front of my dad's eyes, and through gritted teeth, said to my dad, 'If my baby ever sets foot into another boxing ring I am leaving you, and I am taking him with me.' That was the end of my boxing career, temporarily anyway. My dad loved my mom very much, and there is no way he could bear losing one of us let alone both of us. What I cannot get over is my mom calling me her baby, I mean I was five foot ten inches tall and I was 16 years old. But then that was mom.

I said to Mr O'Conner, "mom still refers to me as her baby." Milly piped up, "And my mom says that to me." Mr O'Conner and I looked at each other, and burst into laughter, but Milly was not amused. Milly said, "It's not funny you know, when mom calls me in for tea, she says 'tea's ready baby', in front of all the other guys and girls. I have told her to stop calling me her baby, and she just says 'but you are my baby, aren't you? Yes mom, but not outside. She still does it, it's not funny." Which made us laugh even harder.

Then Milly saw the funny side of it, and joined in laughing with us, when we had stopped laughing. Mr O'Conner said, "I think our moms will always see us as their babies, no matter what." With a serious look on his face, Mr O'Conner said, "Look Oliver, what about your mom? She is going to be worried about you." "It should be ok as I told mom I would be going round to Milly's house after we had been to the sweet shop." I asked him what he did knowing his boxing career was over.

"Well Oliver, I have never told this story before, to anyone. When I left school I became an apprentice carpenter, which meant when I became twenty one, my apprenticeship finished, then I would be classed as a fully skilled carpenter, which I became. I managed to get a job in a factory making furniture, that is where I met my beautiful wife. She worked in the offices there. I instantly fell in love, the minute I set eyes on her I knew she was for me. I happened to see her in town one day, I plucked up the courage and asked her for a date."

"She just looked at me, and said 'no thanks' and walked away. My heart sank, but her friend who was with her, walked back to me, and said, 'My friend Mary, really likes you, but her dad does not particularly like the Irish.' Cutting a long story short we eventually got around that problem. We then started courting, and I promised her that now my apprenticeship is finished, we could get married, and as I promised, six months later we did with the approval of her dad. Eventually Mary got pregnant and we had a beautiful baby girl, and we named her Sarah-Ann."

"We lived with my mom and dad to begin with, but soon realised it wasn't going to work, we needed a place of our own, and with the help of Mary's father, we managed to get a small two-bedroom house, with a reasonable rent. We were really happy there. Using my carpentry skills, we had a nice home, we were really happy, life was good, but as always something always comes along, and spoils things. I had heard rumours that we may be going to war with Germany. This was devastating news, our life was going to be turned upside down. Mary was really worried. She asked me, "Shamus, do you think you will be called up for duty?" "Mary, I honestly do not know."

But within a matter of weeks, war was declared and I was conscripted into the army. At least I managed to share Sarah Ann's third birthday, a few days before I left. It was heart-breaking for me. As the train pulled out of the station seeing them standing there crying. I forced back my tears, I am a man, I am not supposed to cry, but then I turned and looked at some of my fellow soldiers. A few were unashamedly crying, and getting a ribbing for it, then I felt the warm tears rolling down my cheeks, I quickly wiped them away."

Then Mr. O'Conner realised as he was telling this story, to Milly and me, tears were once more rolling down his cheeks, as he recalled this painful memory. "Well what is amazing is you two lads are still awake, after hearing me droning on, but you do appear to be genuinely interested.", 'This is good for me, to get it off my chest I had bottled all these feelings, and anger, inside me, for all these years. Obviously not doing me any good, perhaps as I was their saviour, they are now my saviour.'

Mr O'Conner suddenly said, "Hey guys, I am so sorry for going on and on, it must be boring for you." He then glanced across at Milly. Milly said, "Mr O'Conner we are not bored, we want to know more, we never knew you were a boxer, or even that you were a carpenter." Mr O'Conner then said. "Are you guys sure, you want to hear more?" "Yes, yes," nodding our heads in unison, "we are sure." "Ok then, before I carry on, Milly, if you go to my fridge, you will find a couple of cans of coca cola. For you and Oliver. Oliver, you go and get yourself cleaned up as best you can. If you go upstairs the bathroom is to your left." "Thank you, Mr O'Conner."

As I reached the top of the stairs, I noticed the door directly in front of me was partly open, and I could see what appeared to be a silver ornamental framed photograph, which I guessed must be his wife and daughter. I thought to myself, 'stop being nosey Oliver, go and get cleaned up'. I went to the bathroom door and on opening, was surprised what a nice bathroom it was. I stood in front of the bathroom mirror. As I looked at my reflection in the mirror, I was shocked to see my nose looked slightly flatter and broader than it used to. Seeing the dried blood caked in my nostrils around my mouth and chin, my white school shirt ruined, blood probably won't wash out. God, mom will go crazy, probably be grounded as well. I thought to myself, 'Oliver, what the hell were you thinking?' My stupidity continued, when admonishing myself by hitting my forehead with the heel of my hand 'very painful'.

That is when I realised, that large fist of his must have caught my forehead, as well as my nose, saving my nose from further damage. I looked at my swollen nose, it could have been worse. I suppose if he had caught me fully in the face, I could have an ear to ear nose, which made me chuckle. 'Stop that,' I thought, 'that's what got you into trouble in the first place.'

I do not think he would have punched me if I hadn't started laughing at him. Anyway, time to get myself cleaned up, I managed to wash the blood off my face, but not out of my nostrils. It was too painful. While washing the blood out of the sink, I noticed how male dominated everything was, razor, shaving soap stick, brush, aftershave, single toothbrush in his rinsing cup 'blue' had to be, nothing female to be seen anywhere. Where were his wife and daughter? Perhaps I will find out later. I left the bathroom and walked out onto the landing. As I passed the partly open door, I could not resist looking again into what I presumed was Mr O'Conner's bedroom.

Curiosity got the better of me, and I walked into the bedroom. I glanced around the room, still the same masculine feeling to it, unmade bed, nothing unusual there, except the handle of a baseball bat sticking out from under the bed. Oh well, with neighbours like that, who can blame him, my eyes then focused on what I had actually come into the room to look at, which was the photograph. There was a pendant draped across the top of the picture frame, he had hooked the gold chain over the supporting leg of the picture frame which made the pendant hang over the heads of the two females in the picture, who I presumed to be his wife and daughter.

When I looked at the daughter, there was no mistaking who she belonged to. She was the virtual double of Mr O'Conner; his wife was very pretty with dark hair, set in the styles of that day, as were the dresses they were wearing. The daughter also had dark hair, which had been braided into pigtails, which were hanging forward over her shoulders, with ribbons tied onto them. This was when I noticed the pendant around the girl's neck. The mother had one too and was identical to the daughter's. I returned to the living room, where I found Mr O'Conner chatting to Milly, he was asking Milly about his family, and where they originated from. Milly seemed to be enjoying his chat with Mr O'Conner, and in between 'slurping' on his cola, Milly was a real irritating 'slurper' with all of his drinks, but I cannot help but love that little fella. I waited patiently for them to finish their conversation.

Mr O'Conner then turned to me, and said. "Ah, Oliver that looks better, pity about the shirt though, I think your ma's going to be pretty mad with you." "Well I have already got my excuse worked out, I am going to tell her it was a couple of boys from another school, and they jumped me from behind, knocking me to the floor, and then kicking me in the face, hence my bloody nose. I'll tell her, I caught sight of their uniform as they ran away, but don't know what they looked like. If I tell mom it was Jake and his family, she will go berserk. She will go storming around to their house, and I do not want that, she could get hurt."

"Ok Oliver, do you and Milly want to go home now?" "No, Mr O'Conner, we would like you to tell us the rest of the story you were telling us." Mr O'Conner smiled and said, "Are you sure you're not bored?" "Bored? Definitely not, please carry on. But before you do, can I just ask you about the photograph on your dressing table? You must think I am being a Nosey Parker, but your bedroom door was partly open. I couldn't help but notice the photo as I went to the bathroom. I am guessing it must be your wife and daughter." "Mr O'Conner replied, "Yes it is." I could see the sadness sweep over him as he said it. "Where are they Mr O'Conner? Did you get divorced, or something?"

I had noticed when he was first telling us about his earlier life, it seemed to uplift him, even his eyes seemed to become brighter, but simply mentioning about his wife and daughter, I seemed to have struck a raw nerve somewhere. I said, "I am so sorry Mr O'Conner, I was just curious." He did not say anything, just leaned forward in his chair, head bowed, wringing his hands. I looked across at Milly, who was sitting in a comfy chair that he looked lost in. He just gave me that upward nod of the head and raised eyebrows, which I knew meant had we better go. I was just about to get out of my chair, when Mr O'Conner suddenly looked up, and said,

"Sorry lads, it upsets me when I think about it, and yes to your question, I did get divorced. That was my second marriage, which did not last very long, two years actually. If you remember, I was telling you about my first wife Mary, and my daughter Sarah Ann, and when I was called up to go in the army. You see you have no choice, you have to go out there and kill or be killed. I lost a lot of good friends out there. We were approaching a place called Monte casino in Italy, and the Germans had taken it over. Our mission was to take it back when my best friend trod on a mine, killing him instantly. This mine was full of ball bearings, it was designed to kill and injure as many people as possible. I was one of them and two other soldiers were injured.

My injuries were quite severe, I was hospitalised for about a month. It took about seven weeks before I could walk again, and was eventually sent home on leave to recover. I was shipped back to England, with a lot more badly injured soldiers. Some had lost their sight, some with missing arms and legs, some with no legs at all, their lives were changed forever. I wondered if their wives and children, their parents or sisters and brothers, love them any less or any more, because the people who left these shores to fight the enemy, are not just physically, but must be mentally scarred as well.

That little boy they taught to be caring, and not to hurt anybody, and to respect the laws of the land, now had a rifle thrust into his hands, to forget everything he has been taught, and go and kill as many people as he can, they are never going to be the same again. I have seen terrible things, I will never forget, but at least I was still in one piece. Ok my legs still did not work properly, and my right arm and hand were painful, but in time they would get better. After the ship had docked, I managed to get a lift to the train station, after waiting for nearly half an hour.

I finally boarded the train, managed to get seated by a window, which I was very grateful for ,I just wanted to be alone with my thoughts. As I watched the landscape go by, my thoughts were about when I would be finally reunited with my wife and daughter. I could not wait to see them again, the train journey seemed forever. On arriving at the train station of my hometown, I realised I would have to catch a bus, as there was no way I could have walked to the part of town where I lived, so after another agonising wait for the bus, It came and I was eventually dropped off, three streets from where I lived. It was going to be painful.

But I did not care, even if I had to crawl on my hands and knees , I was going to knock on that door, and see those beautiful faces of my wife and daughter, once again. Once I had got moving it wasn't so bad. My legs had stiffened sitting on the bus for so long. I had only walked a short distance, when I met Mrs Cooper, a neighbour who lived just down the street from us. I said, 'Hello Mrs Cooper, how are you, and how's your husband Bill?' She just looked at me, and said, 'Hello Shamus,' then burst into tears. She pulled out a handkerchief and dabbed her eyes.

I said, 'Mrs Cooper, what is the matter?' She looked at me through teary eyes. 'Is it Bill?' I said to her. She let out a small cry, and said, 'I am so sorry Shamus, I have to go.' She quickly walked past me, and disappeared round the corner. I thought well, that's odd, I am sure Mary would have written and told me, if something had happened to her husband. Oh well, I had better get on, I have still got a bit of a distance to go. I was looking forward to seeing their faces, when they opened the door and they saw me standing there."

Mr O'Conner's stopped telling his story for a moment, because he realised he was going on a bit. He could see Milly was getting a bit bored. He said to Oliver, "There's some chocolate biscuits in the biscuit barrel." Milly jumped up, "Where- where?" "In the kitchen, Milly." Well, except for the crunching that kept him quiet for a while. He said to us, "Look you guys, if you want to go, I'll understand, I can finish telling you the rest another day." "No-no," we both said, "we're ok." "Are you sure, there is not much more to tell you." Then I said, "Please carry on Mr O'Conner." He continued, "So where was I? Oh yes I remember now."

"Anyway, I had almost reached the corner of my street when this big guy came running around the corner, nearly knocking me off my feet, as he ran past me. I recognised him, it was Bill, Mrs Cooper's husband. I shouted, 'Hey Bill, it's me Shamus.' He turned around and looked at me, for a few seconds. There was just a blank stare, then recognition. Then he said, 'Oh my god, Shamus! I am so sorry for nearly knocking you over, I was trying to catch up with Betty, as she has got a Doctor's appointment. She has not been very well, her nerves mostly. It's because of the bombing in the area, besides other things it's really shook her up. Did you know about the bombing in this area, Shamus?' I said, 'No Bill, I knew the Germans had bombed a town about twenty miles from here.'

Then Bill said, 'They have bombed here as well, they have done a lot of damage.' 'Why here?' I asked Bill. 'Well, they seemed to target the foundry, and the steel factory across the river.' 'Did they hit the foundry?' I asked Bill, panicking, because mom and dad both worked there. They are ok,' Bill said, 'they are fine, they were both at home when the bombing started.' I said, 'Oh thank god for that.' Then Bill looked away from me, threw his head back and looked into the sky.

"Bill finally looked at me with tears in his eyes, and with a tremble in his voice, uttered a few words that tore my world apart, he said, 'Christ Shamus, why did it have to be me, that has to tell you?' And deep in the pit of my stomach I knew. I fell backwards against the wall of the house behind me, sliding down into a heap on the pavement, numb with shock. I just couldn't speak, then I heard a voice that seemed far away, it was Bill he had knelt down by the side of me, talking to me, trying to comfort me.

"Still in a daze, I looked at Bill, 'Please tell me not both of them.' He didn't speak, just nodded his head. That Oliver and Milly was the end of my world. Sorry if I called you Milly, your name is Rueben, isn't it?" Milly answered with a smile, "Yes, it is Mr O'Conner, but I am Milly to my friends, you can call me Milly, if you want to." That seemed to touch Mr O'Conner, he told us he did not have many friends, young or old, the only real friend he had was his next door neighbour, Jack. He had been in the army with him, and had been close friends, ever since they came out of the army together, but they had fallen out about a year and a half ago, over some broken fencing, and he had lost his Irish temper again, and had regretted it afterwards. He tried to apologise, but Jack did not want to know.

He said life had become very lonely, and he was so grateful that 'you two wonderful kids would want to even bother listening to me.' Oliver noticed Mr O'Conner suddenly became quite serious, and with a troubled look on his face, said, "I have something to tell you, it's a secret that we must keep to ourselves," in almost a whisper. I said, "Ok Mr O'Conner, looking over at Milly, "we can keep a secret."

Mr O'Conner leaned forward in his chair, and said, "Look you guys, I am trusting the two of you, not to tell anyone." I wondered, is he going to give us a map, to the pot of gold at the end of the rainbow? Well he is Irish. Brain to 'Stupid Oliver, just listen.' Mr O'Conner then told us something totally unexpected, which shocked us both, very deeply. This kind man told us he had been suffering from blinding headaches for a number of years, but finally decided to go and see his doctor. After he had dizzy spells and a couple of blackouts, his doctor sent Mr O'Conner to the hospital for tests.

On seeing his doctor for the results, his doctor had told him the worst possible news - that he had a malignant brain tumour. And that it was inoperable, worse still, was that he had only six to nine months to live, twelve if he is lucky. The doctor had told him to expect vision and memory problems, eventually losing the ability to walk, and will need looking after. The doctor asked if he had any close relatives who could help him, Mr O'Conner replied, "No I have nobody." We were so shocked by what he told us, we were speechless.

There was an awkward silence, for about thirty seconds, then in a firm voice, I said, "Mr O'Conner you can rely on us, we will help you. We can run errands for you, fetch groceries, anything you want just tell us, we can drop it on the way from school, but Mr O'Conner we will have to tell our moms." He thought for a while, then said, "Ok, kids tell your mothers, but tell them to keep it to themselves. Anyway I am ok for the time being, so do not worry yourselves for now."

I surprised myself by asking him, considering what had happened in his life, did he believe in god, and if he believed in heaven and hell, like the bible says? He told me he was brought up as a strict Catholic. But what has happened to him throughout his life, and seeing the horrors of war, made him question his faith. "Well Oliver, I can only hope there is a heaven, son, I believe we are already in hell. This is it, right here and now." I did not ask anymore. Then Milly piped up, "Mr O'Conner, I hope you don't mind me asking, but did you ever go back to your house?" "Yes, Rueben I did, I had nowhere to live, so I moved in with mom and dad, and it was only my mom, persuading me to go and see the house before it was demolished.

"It was heart-breaking for both of us, we were crying and hugging each other, as we looked at the wreck that used to be my family home. What convinced me to come to the house was mom could see how devastated I was, and she gave me a stern but gentle lecture, making me realise I was not the only one hurting. She said just remember, 'I have lost a beautiful granddaughter, you know, whom I absolutely adored. And losing a kind gentle soul, Mary, my daughter in law, my best friend. Somebody I could always rely on,' she said, 'your father is absolutely heart broken, and cannot bring himself to visit the house.'

"Mom had told me that sixteen people, in my street, had been killed, that included two whole families who were wiped out. In one of those families, was my daughter's best friend, Jessica, who was the same age as Sarah-Ann. Anyway, we wiped our tears away, and I had decided to try and get into what was left of my house. Mom told me that I was stupid, as it could collapse in on me, but I was determined to see whether I could find something that belonged to my family, no matter how small or insignificant it may be. I managed to get about six feet into the building, on my hands and knees. Cutting my hand on a piece of glass, I quickly wrapped my hand up with my handkerchief. I soon realised I wasn't going to get anywhere, as the fire and the bombs had done so much damage, so I decided to reverse out still on my hands and knees.

About halfway out, I noticed a piece of plaster, which had obviously fallen off one of the walls, it was about a foot in diameter. I was about to leave it undisturbed, when something just told me to lift it up. I picked it up, and turned it over. And there, pinned to the plaster was a drawing, in crayon, depicting me with my arms outstretched in front of me, with Sarah Ann and Mary running towards me. I just lay there in the dust and dirt, my emotions overwhelming me. Then I heard mom calling to me, 'Shamus, are you alright? I know what you are looking for, you will not find it. She knew I was looking for my daughter's locket, as I had given my wife and daughter identical lockets, in which I had inserted a small black and white photograph of myself. And they were distinctive by a red cross that was on the front of the locket.

"The fireman who attended to the fires in the street had said they had only found the one locket on the adult female. They said the fire was so fierce, it is a wonder they found anything at all. They said the only reason they found the locket was because a beam had fallen across the adult female's chest, protecting the locket. They believe the young female was definitely killed by the incendiary device, and the locket could have melted in the intense heat. They believe the adult female was killed by falling masonry from the bomb that struck the house a short time later.

"Mom's voice broke through my thoughts. 'Shamus, please come out, it's dangerous in there.' 'Ok mom, I am on my way, I have something to show you.' When finally I did get out from the rubble, I held what I had found in front of me, with the back of the plaster towards her. She looked at it, then looked at me, a piece of plaster. 'I don't think so,' she said. 'But mom, it's from the kitchen wall, I don't care where it's from.' 'That's ridiculous.' Then I turned it round. The look on my mom's face was priceless, she took a sharp intake of breath.

'Now I understand, oh how wonderful!' But this is a strange thing, because our next door neighbour but one, who was a plasterer by trade, I had asked if he would plaster my kitchen walls for me. This was about six months before I was called up for the army. He agreed and did a first class job, he was a good friend and neighbour, and when I offered to pay him, he just completely refused, and would not let me give him anything at all. Laughing, he just said, 'Perhaps one day, you can do some carpentry for me.' I said, 'That is no problem at all.'

I thanked him, and asked if he and his family would like to come round for tea, so Les and his family came around to our house, where I met his wife, and his young daughter, who was the same age as Sarah Ann. They got on really well, and she would come round, quite regularly, to play with Sarah

Ann. His wife Sheila was a nice quiet woman. Their daughter Elizabeth, was the complete opposite, she was a friendly bubbly little girl. So, what I was holding in my hands, was the creation of two people I will never see again. My good friend Les, was killed in France, I learned from Bob. My neighbour across the street, a bomb had hit the Thorpe family home, killing Sheila and Elizabeth.

On my way back to mom and dad's house, I attempted to take the drawing pins out of the picture, and separate it from the plaster, but when mom saw what I was doing, she stopped me, and said, 'Leave it exactly how it is, you have part of your daughter and part of her home, keep them together.' So dad made a picture frame, cutting the plaster to the same size as the picture, putting glass on the front to protect it. While dad was in his shed making the frame, mom said, 'Take him a cup of tea, as he has been in there all day,' but as I approached the shed I could hear him sobbing.

I had not got the heart to go into the shed to see him, on hearing him, I broke down myself. Hey you guys, if you look to the right of the front door, you will see my daughter's picture, and the frame my dad made. I put it there to remind me God giveth but God also taketh away, I detected a slight bitterness in his voice.

I said to Mr O'Conner, "We have to go now anyway, we will have a look at the picture before we go." So we both got out of our chairs, and made our way to the door. We both had a look at the picture, and were surprised, for a six-year old, it was really good. I said she looked as if she was quite talented, in a quiet voice he answered, "She was."

Mr O'Conner said, "She took after me, I do paintings myself. I have about thirty paintings and one day I will show them to you." I said, "Why haven't you put them on your walls?" He replied, "I don't think they are good enough to hang on walls, anyway they are not framed." After he told me that, I could not wait to see his paintings.

We were standing by the door when Mr O'Conner got up off his chair. As he approached the door, Milly suddenly said, "Mr O'Conner, could I use your toilet, please?" "Yes of course, you can." While Milly was doing what he needed to do, Mr O'Conner said, "Oliver, have a look at the plaque on the other side of the doorway." About the same height as the picture on the other side of the doorway was a ceramic plaque. It was about 8"x9" square, white, with a shamrock in each corner. There were words written on it, in large letters at the top. It read,

IRELAND

An old Irish blessing

May the road rise to meet you

May the wind be always at your back

The sun shine warm upon your face

The rainfall soft upon your fields

And until we meet again

May god hold you in the hollow of his hand

"The words are absolutely beautiful," I said to Mr O'Conner, he smiled and said, "We Irish sometimes have our moments." I smiled in agreement, then Milly joined us at the doorway, I thanked Mr O'Conner, for rescuing me. "No, thank you for your company, and listening to me, I did tend to go on a bit though." Then Milly said, "You didn't tell us why the horrible Garnett family are so frightened of you." "Ok, I'll tell you quickly then you will have to go. A few months ago, I was walking down the street where they live. I could hear raised voices coming from the Garnetts' house.

The next thing I know, Mrs Garnett came running out of her front door, followed by her husband Reg, who was bawling his head off, at her. He grabbed her, and threw her against the wall of the house, I heard the thud, as her head struck the wall. He was shouting at her, 'I told you I wanted steak tonight, you stupid bitch.' I could feel my Irish temper building inside me like a volcano, but first I needed to see if Mrs Garnett was ok. I helped her up off the floor, and asked if she was ok, she said, 'Thank you I am alright.' I said, 'Go inside your house.'

She looked up at me with big sad eyes. I never realised how pretty she was, even with a cut and swollen lip, and a black eye. My volcano was about to erupt. 'But he will hurt you,' she whispered. 'No, he won't. Go in the house." She did as I asked, then Reg the slob, as I call him, growled at me, 'You will be sorry, I am now going to have to hurt you badly. You should learn to mind your own business, Paddy,' as he advanced towards me. Punching his clenched fist into the palm of his left hand, he spat out at me, 'Hope you like hospital food.' He did not know how ironic those words would be.

When he was about two feet away from me, he stopped, grinning, showing his nicotine stained teeth, 'You're going down, Paddy.' Now I am about five feet ten inches tall, this loud mouthed bully, was easily six feet two or three inches tall, probably weighed about twenty stone, so he was a big guy, but he did not realise he was facing a very angry Irishman. The next thing I know, he takes a huge swing at me, I ducked just in time, as his huge fist sailed over the top of my head, then my volcanic temper fully erupted. My fists were so tightly clenched, they felt like two lumps of rock, after his swing at me, it left his gut fully exposed.

So I drove my left fist into it, I heard him grunt as my fist landed, then I drove my right fist into his ribs, I heard him scream in pain, but I wasn't finished yet. When I was boxing they used to call my right hand sledgehammer, as I knocked nearly all my opponents out with it, so I got the nickname, sledgehammer O'Conner. I sensed he was about to fall, so before he did, I gave him a final sledgehammer to the jaw. I thought I heard a crack as my fist connected. He went down, almost as if in slow motion, as if I had cut a big tree down, then his two sons came running out of the house. Jake screamed at me, 'What have you done to my dad?' 'Nothing he did not deserve.'

Jake started to advance towards me, but my volcano was still in full flow, so if I had to take on the two sons as well, I was still angry enough to do it. Luckily for Jake, he looked at his dad, then looked at me, and realised it may not be the best thing to do. I said to his other son, 'Gary, you had better get an ambulance for your father.' He nodded and said ok. I then went on to do my shopping, volcano subsiding with every footstep. Jake screamed after me, 'You will pay for this.' Ok Milly I think that may be why they are scared of me."

We both stood there with our mouths open, then Milly just said, "Wow." Please remember kids I am not telling you to be violent but sometimes you have no choice. We said goodbye to Mr O'Conner. As I was going, I quietly said, "I'll tell mom our secret, and me and Milly, will come and see you as soon as we can." "Ok Oliver, see you." With that he went inside and closed the door.

As we were passing Mr O'Conner's neighbour Jack, whom he had fallen out with, his door suddenly opened, and Jack appeared on the doorstep. He said, "Hello Oliver." I said, "Hello." Jack said, "I heard the commotion down the alleyway, was it that damned Garnett family again?" I said, "Yes it was." He said, "I can see the blood on your shirt, what happened? I told him, we were fed up with being bullied, so I had decided to stand up to them, especially Jake, as he is the worst bully. Jack said, "I saw Shamus run past my window, and I wondered what was going on, I stood on my doorstep and watched, it was comical to see those Garnetts fall over themselves, to get away from Shamus. They are terrified of him, he has had a run in with them before." I noticed we were speaking very quietly, obviously we did not want Mr O'Conner to hear us.

Jack said the Garnetts did not know who he was, to them he was just an old Irishman. Jack started chuckling, he put his hand to his mouth, to try and stifle the noise he was making. "Well they certainly know who he is now," Jack said. "Did you know he used to be a boxer, and his nickname used to be sledgehammer? "Yes," I replied, "Mr O'Conner told us all about it." "Right so is he ok? We had a bit of a fall out, and we don't speak to each other," Jack said, "do you know he is the kindest, most generous man I have ever met, but stubborn and quick tempered, you cross him, you had better run fast.

Shamus may be getting on a bit, but for his age, he really is a fit strong man. He built a large shed, in his backyard, where he has made himself a small gym. He has weights, exercise machines, everything. I would hear him about 6 o'clock in the morning, go to his gym. After about ten minutes, I would hear him on his punch bag. After a couple of hours, it would go quiet. He had made the other half of his shed, into a studio where he does his painting. He is a brilliant artist, but he does not think that he is, I have told him to have an exhibition, but Shamus being Shamus does not want to know.

"I have not heard or seen Shamus, go to his shed to exercise or paint for months, do you know if he is alright?" I thought to myself, oh god what do I do, he obviously cares about Mr O'Conner, do I tell him? Well I am already going to tell mom. I think he should really know, so I whispered to him, "Please do not tell Mr O'Conner, I have told you this, I do not want to make him angry." "I don't think either of us want that," Jack said, smiling when he said it. The smile soon disappeared, when I told him how seriously ill he was, and what short time he had left, the smile had turned to shock and disbelief.

The colour had drained from Jack's face, he was as white as a sheet. Jack said, "Thank you," then there was a long pause, and finally said, "Thank you Oliver. I have to go." With that, he quickly went inside and closed the door. He was clearly shaken by what I had told him. Then I heard Milly's voice close to my ear, "Ooooh you're in trouble, you told a secret you're not supposed to tell." "Shut up Milly, I had to tell him. Anyway, why were you in the bathroom? You are usually jet propelled in and out in about thirty seconds."

Milly took a quick look behind him. "I happened to go into Mr O'Conner's bedroom. I had a quick look at the photo on his dresser, his daughter looks just like him, and I was curious about that locket, after he told us about the photo inside it, so I opened it and had a look inside, there is a photo inside, when he was younger and in the army." Also a picture of a young girl, "Milly you snoop." "Okay Oliver, I know, I should not have done it, I just could not help myself," Milly said, "Did you notice how untidy his house is?" "Well, he is a man, we are not supposed to be tidy are we? It's just a man thing. Milly, we had better get running." We ran through the alley, as fast as we could, luckily no sign of the Garnetts. It was summertime, so mom used to let me stay out a bit longer because of the lighter nights. But when I walked through the door, and she saw all the blood on my shirt, she said, "Oh my god, what has happened to you, are you alright?" I said, "Mom I am ok, some boys, I guess maybe from another school, jumped on me, and before I could do anything, punched me in the nose." "Do you know who they are, would you recognise them?" "No mom, I have not got a clue who they are."

I managed to talk mom into not going to the police, she was even talking about going down to school. I said to mom, "I do not know who they were, so there is no point." She said, "Alright, just promise me you will be more careful." I said, "Ok mom, I will." Mom said, "Oh, I was just thinking, where was Rueben, when this was happening?" "Oh oh, Milly you mean. "Yes Milly, as you call him," mom said. "Oh, he had gone on in front, and didn't see anything." "I just wondered that's all." Phew, that was close, the last thing I want is mom to find out what really happened, else she would go storming around there, and get herself hurt.

I waited till mom had made a cup of tea, and sat down. "Mom, I have something to tell you, I have promised someone that I would keep this a secret, but I am allowed to tell you." "Ok spill the beans, on the secret then," mom said with a wry smile, not realising what I was about to tell her. I told her, it was Mr O'Conner, who frightened those boys off, and how he let me use his bathroom to wash the blood off my face. I told her how ill he is, and the short time he has left. He has no family and nobody to look after him, so I promised him, me and Milly would pop in from school, and run any errands he might need." Mom said, "That's ok, I have met Mr O'Conner, and he seems like a really nice man, tell him if there is anything I can do, to let me know."

Well, mom being mom, went to his house the next day, and although he protested, mom cooked him a meal, and tidied up for him. He told mom that he was ok for the moment but mom was having none of it. The next day was Sunday, mom cooked our Sunday dinner, but I noticed there were three plates. Puzzled at first, it clicked she had asked Mr O'Conner round for dinner. Mom had asked him to

Sunday dinner, he told mom he was not feeling too good, he said perhaps another time. Stubborn as ever, mom said, "If the mountain won't come to Mohammed, Mohammed will have to go to the mountain." I said, "What?" "Don't "what" me Oliver, it is a famous saying, I am trying to be clever here."

She had that silly grin on her face, "Well Oliver, you are Mohammed today, and Mr O'Conner is the mountain. I am putting a plate over the top of Mr O'Conner's dinner and wrapping a couple of tea towels around it. I want you to take the dinner to Mr O'Conner. Remember Oliver, we have to help this man while we can, we do not know how long he has left." "I know mom, and I don't mind." "You do realise, Oliver, you are a very special boy, and a very kind boy." I am so proud of you. I set off to Mr O'Conner's, dinner burning my hands. I eventually got there, hot gravy trickling between my fingers, balancing the dinner on one hand, I knocked on the door, the door opened, and it was Jack standing there. "Hello Oliver, it's ok you have come to the right house. Let me take that off you, come in."

I sat down opposite Mr O'Conner, he was fast asleep, even me knocking on the door had not woken him up. Jack put the dinner on the kitchen table. He said in a whisper, "Shamus did not sleep very well last night, he is exhausted. He dropped off while I was talking to him. I am going to leave him for a bit longer, then I will wake him for his dinner." I said to Jack, "Are you friends again?" Jack said, "Yes, we are, thank goodness. After what you had told me, I arrived on his doorstep with a bottle of Irish whiskey, an offer he could not refuse."

Jack laughed at this, then his face took on a more serious look, as he looked at his friend asleep in his chair. Jack sighed, and said, "I don't know what I am going to do, when he has gone. My wife died a few years ago, and although I have two children, my daughter lives in France, and my son lives in Australia. I talk to them on the phone, every week. They have both asked me to go and live with them, I say, 'no thank you, this is my home, England'." Until mom had told me, I didn't know Jack's surname. She said it's Mr Weaver. He is totally different to Mr O'Conner, he is short and stocky, with thinning grey hair, a round face, with a ruddy complexion and very pale blue eyes. Every time I have met him, he always speaks to me and has a smile on his face, but today more of a frown. "I have to go Mr Weaver, mom's waiting with my dinner." "Ok Oliver, I will watch you go down through the alleyway, just to make sure the Garnetts are not about, I said thank you Mr Weaver, bye."

Well I got home safely. Mom continued popping in to see Mr O'Conner, cooking him an occasional meal, and Jack continued going around every day. About a week had passed, the Garnetts continued to leave us alone, but the bullies at school still carried on their bullying, always picking on the smallest and weakest. I thought to myself, one day the shoe will be on the other foot, but except for the bullying, I love school, and so does Milly. I am top of my class in science, maths and art, I seem to excel at almost everything, mom says she is so proud of me. Milly is top of his class, in maths, English and geography. My science teacher Mr Gough said I am like a sponge, I soak everything up.

On the sad side though, my brilliant art teacher, Mr Cheadle, is leaving this Friday. We were told in assembly, the new art teacher is Mrs Addison, and she starts next Monday.

Nothing exciting was happening in mine and Milly's life at the moment. We went down the park, me and Milly played football, nearly all day. Milly's not the best at sports, we were playing five a side, Milly could not kick a ball to save his life, so we put him in goal. Big mistake, we lost eight to one. Not to worry, we bought a big bottle of orange pop, and some chocolate from a local shop, so it wasn't all bad.

On Sunday, me and mom went to the funeral of a neighbour of ours, she lived three doors down from us. Mom said she was a horrible woman, foul mouthed and bad tempered. I said, "Mom, why are we going if she was such a nasty person?" Mom answered, "Respect, just respect, Oliver." While we were in the church, I happened to look around, and only counted about six people there, and I think that included the vicar. I felt sorry for the woman, nasty or not, I wonder what our new neighbours will be like.

For Art's Sake

Monday happened to be a good day, warm and sunny, as me and Milly made our way to school, walking through the alleyway. My only thought was Jake, 'is he waiting for us?' I pushed that out of mind, as I passed a huge lilac tree that was hanging over the wall of somebody's garden, the scent was beautiful. I also caught the scent of a privet tree that must have been left to grow and blossom. I loved anything like that, but Milly thought it was rather 'girly'. Anyway we arrived at school, without any problems. Strange, we did not get bullied in the playground either, had we suddenly become invisible? Oh well, perhaps this could turn out to be a really good day, most of the lessons were my favourites, such as science and maths.

Last lesson of the day is art, with the new teacher. After our dinner break, I was walking down the school corridor, with Milly. We were going back to our class rooms, when Milly said, "Look, it's the new art teacher." She was coming towards us from the head master's office. As she came closer, Milly nudged me in the ribs, with his elbow, "Look Oliver. She has a locket exactly the same, as the one on the picture frame." Luckily for me she had stopped a short distance away from us, to talk to another teacher, which then gave me the opportunity to get a closer look at Miss Addison's locket. As they were standing close to the doorway to my classroom, I could patiently wait, until they had finished talking, and I did get a better look at the locket.

Milly was right, it was identical to the one draped across the picture frame, with the photographs of Mr O'Conner's wife and daughter, both wearing the same locket, as the one I am looking at now. She stopped talking and looked at me, and said, "Hello." I said, "Hello." I had only fleetingly looked at her before, now she was looking directly at me. It was like Mr O'Conner's legendary sledgehammer punches hitting me.

As I looked into her face, this had to be his daughter, the resemblance was uncanny, the same eyes-nose-mouth, even the smile, but it was the eyes that convinced me more than anything. Both artists as well. It's too much of a coincidence. It had to be her, how and why I do not know. I felt my teacher, shaking me by my shoulder, and saying, "Wakey, wakey Oliver. I was just telling Miss Addison what a clever student you are." "Oh sorry, miss, I was miles away." "You are in Miss Addison's art class later." I replied, "Yes miss, last lesson." "Oh right, Oliver, I will see you in class later then." I replied, "Yes miss." With that she said 'bye and continued down the corridor, passing Milly who just stood there with his mouth wide open.

As she passed him she said, "Hello." Milly was absolutely dumb founded, and did not answer at first. She said to him, "Are you alright?" Milly said, "Yes miss, sorry, er hello." She just smiled at him, then carried on down the corridor, eventually disappearing into her classroom. I was in a turmoil for the rest of the afternoon, my teacher Miss Keats asked if there was anything wrong. She said, "When you came into the classroom you were pale, as if you had seen a ghost. Smiling at her I said, "I think I may have." With a puzzled look on her face, she said you may be coming down with something, just let me know if you're not feeling too good I will let you go home." "Oh, no, no miss I am feeling fine." "Ok then, Oliver."

She walked back to her desk. I thought to myself that the last thing I need is to go home. I have to ask Miss Addison where she had got the locket from although deep down I already knew how she had come by it. The afternoon dragged on, seemingly forever. I had very mixed emotions about this, asking Miss Addison things that must be quite personal to her and may end up upsetting her.

But I know I have to do this. The only thing was doubt had started to creep in, because Mr O'Conner was so sure that his wife and daughter had died in that bombing raid, in world war two. He had told me that the fireman had found the remains of an adult female and they believe the remains of a young female. Could they have been mistaken? Because if I am wrong I could be upsetting two people, and one who is seriously ill. I would never forgive myself if I upset Mr O'Conner but it is a risk I have to take because the upside is.

I may be able to reunite a father with his daughter and how wonderful that would be, "Believe in yourself, Oliver." That voice seemed as if it was in my head, but it did not sound like me. Oh well, a bit creepy though. As I am making my way down the school corridor to my last lesson of the day, which is the art class with Miss Addison, thoughts were racing through my mind, I would have to wait till class was finished before I could talk to her, also how am I going to approach her about such a delicate subject? But like the voice said, I have to believe in myself. So I waited till the last of my classmates had gone. I steeled myself and approached Miss Addison's desk. She was a very attractive woman, as far as I could tell she had this flawless pale skin, deep blue eyes and jet black hair tied back into a ponytail. I think maybe I should ask her to marry me. Hello brain to Oliver she Is your teacher, STUPID complete your mission,

She suddenly looked up and said, "Oh, Oliver isn't it?" I gulped and said, "Yes miss." She said, "Is there anything I can help you with? "Actually there is. I don't know how to ask you this, I hope you will not be offended." She stopped writing and sat back in her chair, she pushed her spectacles back on to the bridge of her nose. They had obviously slipped down, while she was writing. With a smile she said, "Ok Oliver, ask away." I gulped again, and said, "Can you please tell me how you came by your locket?"

Her smile disappeared. She leaned forward on her desk and looked me in the eye, and said, "My locket, Oliver?" "Yes miss." She said "Why would you be interested in my locket?" I said, "Because I happen to know where there is another one exactly the same as yours miss." She turned her head and looked out of the classroom window, after a short time she turned back to me. At first she did not say anything, then she said, "Look Oliver, I detected a slight anger in her voice, I could see she was trying to compose herself. There was a pause, then she said something I had not anticipated.

She very sternly said, "With the greatest of respect Oliver, you just do not go around asking personal questions to people you hardly know, especially your teacher." "I, I am very sorry miss, I didn't mean to upset you." "I think you had better go home Oliver, now." With that I quickly left the classroom. I met Milly in the playground where he had been patiently waiting for me. "Well, did you ask her?" "Yes Milly I did, she just does not want to know." "Oh," Milly said, "I did not expect that." "Let's go home Mil, race you to the end of the alley way."

When passing Mr O'Conner's house on the way I had a tinge of guilt and sadness, that I had failed him. It would have hopefully given him some happiness, in the short time he had left, at least I tried. When I got home, I had only just walked through the door, when I heard mom's voice from somewhere in the house, "Oliver what do you want for tea?" I replied, "Nothing mom." Silence, then a loud "What?" from somewhere upstairs. "I'm not hungry mom." She came downstairs, she walked up to me, and put her hand on my forehead, "Well, at least you haven't got a temperature. What is the matter Oliver?" Well, I told her everything.

I told mom about the lockets, and about the uncanny likeness of Miss Addison to Mr O'Conner. Mom said, "You must not upset yourself, you did your best. Sometimes things don't always work out how you expect them to." Mom had just finished speaking, when there was a loud knock at the door. Mom said, "Are you expecting Rueben, Oliver?" "No mom," I replied. She said, "I wonder who this can be then."

Mom opened the door, it was Mrs Addison, I heard her say, "Hello I'm Oliver's art teacher, I'm sorry to bother you." Mom said, "That's alright, come on in. Oliver's told me all about you. Mrs Addison isn't it?" She replied, "Yes it is, I have actually come to apologise to Oliver. I am afraid I was rather sharp with him earlier today." Mom said, "Go on through, Oliver's in the living room." She said 'thank-you', and walked into the living room. I was already standing waiting for her. As she walked into the room, she said, "Hello Oliver, I must apologise for the way I spoke to you earlier." I said, "Look miss, there is no need to apologise, it should be me, that is saying sorry to you, I should not have approached you like I did."

Mom stood in the doorway and said, "Please sit down, Miss Addison," adding, "would you like a cup of tea?" "Yes please," she replied, "milk, one sugar please." Mom disappeared in to the kitchen. Miss Addison turned to me, and said, "Oliver, you mentioned another locket." "Yes miss, I know where there is another exactly the same as yours, I have never seen any others like them. It's the cross on the front of the locket, the little red stones that make up the cross, make it very distinctive." She said, "I have no knowledge of another locket like mine. Do you have the locket?" "No miss," I replied, "but I can take you to the person whom it belongs to. Anyway, I can prove to you of its existence."

Just then mom came in, with our cups of tea, mom set the tray down on our coffee table, and sat in her armchair, sipping her tea, watching and listening intently to us. I said to Miss Addison, "Your locket opens, doesn't it?" "Why, yes Oliver." She prepared to open the locket, I quickly put my hand up and said, "No, no don't open it." She looked at me, a puzzled expression on her face. I said to her, "I believe I can tell you what is in your locket." She said, "Ok Oliver, tell me." With my heart racing I said there are two photographs, one of a dark-haired man in army uniform, the other of a young girl, she also has dark hair. She just stared at me, with wide eyes, then she looked down, when she finally looked up again I could see tears welling up in her eyes.

She started to sob, mom came over to comfort her, and with tears running down her face, she said to me, "Oliver, you know where my mother and father are, don't you? Can you tell me anymore?" "Miss, if you do not mind, I would rather take you to someone who can explain far better than I can about the things that you need to know." "Very good, Oliver. I know I can trust you, will you please not tell anyone, especially at school, till I have sorted things out?"

Mom said, "That is not a problem, we will not mention anything to anyone." Then Miss Addison said, "This is ridiculous at my age, a teacher breaking down in front of a pupil and his mom, foolishly getting my hopes up. But in my defence, you have to understand, I have been searching for my family most of my life. To find them would be absolutely wonderful. To think I could see my mother and father hoping they are still alive." As she said this she looked directly at me, then mom, searching our faces for any signs confirming whether her parents are still with us or not.

Whether she detected anything in our facial expressions, she did not say. But suddenly she seemed to cheer up, and with a tearful smile, she said, "You know I might even have brothers and sisters." I said, "Yes miss, it is quite possible." I thought to myself, I am not lying because I can't remember whether Mr O'Conner had mentioned anything about children from his second marriage.

I then said, "Miss Addison, how did you become separated from your family?" Then mom said, "Oliver, please." "It's alright Mrs Moon, I don't mind, I can only tell you what I can remember, that is before the age of around six or seven years old. I cannot remember anything at all, I don't even know how old I really am. I have a vague memory of wandering around some dark streets, my head was hurting. I put my hand to the back of my head. When I withdrew my hand and looked at it, it was covered in blood. I started to panic, but worse still I could hear what must have been bombs exploding but were very muffled, I realised I could not hear properly."

"Panicking I started to run, it was dark, no street lights and it was raining heavily. I remember running and falling a few times, and totally exhausted, not knowing where I was, I sat down, in what must have been a shop doorway. I sat there for I don't know how long, shivering, soaking wet; then I heard heavy footsteps. I was terrified. The footsteps would stop every so often but were definitely getting closer. I could see a glow in the distance. I thought something must be on fire, then suddenly a dark silhouette appeared in front of me. Before I could scream, a man's soft voice said 'Hello luv, are you alright?' As he leaned forward I realised it was a policeman. He said, 'What's your name?' I said, 'I don't know.' 'Do you know where you live?' I tried to think, but it was just a blank, I said, 'No, I don't know.' He said, 'Come on, I'll take you down to the station.' In those days policemen wore capes, and he wrapped it around me, then he picked me up and carried me to the police station.

"On the way he was talking to me, obviously trying to comfort me. He said, 'I am Paul by the way, and what is… oh, sorry, I forgot, you can't remember.' He laughed and said, 'Silly me, forget my head if it was loose.' He made me laugh, he had one of those silly bristly moustaches that reminded me of a yard brush. That same kind policeman, after visiting his police station, told his sergeant he was taking me to his home, and would bring me back in the morning, his family were very kind to me, his daughter lent me some pyjamas, the policeman's wife treated the cut on the back of my head, which wasn't as bad as I thought, they fed me, and I shared the daughter's bed with her. The next morning I had breakfast with them. My clothes had dried overnight, so I got dressed, I thanked his family for their kindness then we made our way back to the police station.

The policeman said, 'Just sit on the bench, I'll be back in a minute.' I could hear them talking in the other room, I could hear the sergeant telling my policeman friend that he had orders to evacuate all children, no exceptions, that means your daughter as well Paul. 'Sorry,' I heard him groan. He came out to me, he said, 'I am sorry luv, but I have to take you to the coach, they are loading right now, there will be lots of other children, you will be ok.' 'But where are they going to take me?' I asked. He said, 'I don't know, but it will be safer than here.' Well, after travelling for hours, I ended up on a farm, with three other girls. It was hard work on the farm, but we were well fed and well looked after. The other girls eventually went back to their homes, when the war ended."

Of course I had nowhere to go, and my memory of missing years did not return, so as far as anybody knew, I was just another war orphan, so the people who owned the farm, a Mr and Mrs Addison, took me in. When I first arrived at the farm, they asked me my name. I said, 'I cannot remember.' Mrs Addison was a really nice lady. She said, "You poor, dear, we have to call you something. Well what name would you like us to call you?' I thought for a while, and said, 'I don't know why, I like the name Ruth.' 'Lovely dear, Ruth it is.' That is how I came by my first name. My surname is Addison, because I married their son, John Addison. I asked Mrs Addison how she came to be an art teacher. She said, the Addisons, one Christmas, gave me a present of a sketchbook and pencils, and every chance I had, I'd be sketching. Mrs Addison said she believed I had a talent, and she encouraged me to go to college, and one thing led to another, and I became an art teacher.'

Mrs Addison drank her tea, which must have been cold, but she didn't seem to care. She said, "Oliver, is it possible to see this person now?" I replied, "Yes miss, if that is what you want?" "Please," she said, so we all stood up. Mom said, "Is it alright if I come along with you?" Mrs Addison said, "Of course it is."

So we set off on our short journey to Mr O'Conner's, part of our path takes us through the alleyway, hoping the Garnetts are not about. I said, "Mom, I will just go on ahead ok." "Oh yes, of course," mom replied, "you go on." I ran in front, I had to get to Mr O'Conner's, to warn him that mom and Mrs Addison were on their way. When I left them they were chatting away, you would think they had known each other all their lives. I reached Mr O'Conner's, and knocked on his door, a voice from inside said, "Come in, the door's unlocked."

I opened the door and went in. I said, "It is only me, Mr O'Conner." As you entered through the front door, you were greeted by the back of Mr O'Conner's head, and back of his armchair, so he couldn't see me, till I was at the side or in front of his chair. As soon as he saw me he greeted me with a cheery "Hello Oliver." "Mr O'Conner, mom is bringing somebody to see you." "Oh yes, Oliver, who is this person then?" "I cannot tell you, I am just hoping it will be a big and good surprise for you." I could not believe I was saying this, "Mr O'Conner, how is your heart?" He frowned, and looked at me, "Heart, Oliver?" He started to laugh, "It's my head, Oliver, not my heart, I have a problem with." He was still laughing when there was a knock at the door.

I answered the door and, as expected, it was mom and Mrs Addison. "Tell them to come in, Oliver," Mr O'Conner said, as he stood to greet them, in his soft Irish brogue, he said "Hello Alice, and who is this lady?" Mom replied, "This is Ruth, Ruth Addison." He said, "Hello Ruth, pleased to meet you." "And me to meet you, Mr O'Conner." "Please just call me Shamus." She replied, "Ok, if that is alright with you." He just smiled and nodded his head. This was not the response I had expected, although she seemed very nervous, taking quick glances at Mr O'Conner. I know she was trying to work out, 'is this my father?' There did not seem to be any reaction at all from Mr O'Conner. I seem to remember him saying how his eyesight had deteriorated, he thought, due to the tumour, perhaps that is why he has not recognised anything familiar about her.

To me and mom it was as plain as the nose on your face, (ha, pun intended). Mom had sat directly in front of Mr O'Conner, while Mrs Addison had sat on the settee to his left.

Mr O'Conner said, "What can I help you with?" Well, mom is really clever so and so, she said, "Shamus, it is Ruth that needs to talk to you. Ruth, come and sit in my chair, and let me take your coat." It had not dawned on me because she had her coat on, Mr O'Conner would not see the pendant around Mrs Addison's neck, mom had solved both problems in one fell swoop, clever mom. They were now closer to each other, perhaps one or the other will recognise something.

We waited with bated breath, then Mr O'Conner leaned forward, and said, "Ruth do I know you from somewhere, you seem familiar?" With tears in her eyes, she said, "Yes, I believe we knew each other a long time ago." With that she held the pendant she had around her neck in front of him. There was a sharp intake of breath from Mr O'Conner, he quickly stood up, in an angry voice, he said, "Where did you get that from?" In almost a whisper, with tears running down her face, she said, "I believe it was a gift you gave to me, when I was a little girl." She stood up, and said, "Look at me." He looked into her face. She said, "The reason I seem familiar to you is because I am convinced that I am your daughter."

She then took the pendant from around her neck, opened it, and said, "That man in the photograph is you, isn't it? And I know the little girl is me." With anger still in his voice, he said, "Oliver, will you please fetch my glasses off my bedside table?" I quickly ran upstairs, my heart beating fast, I thought to myself, 'God, have I done the right thing here? Well there's no turning back now.' I could hear mom trying to calm things down. So, I found his glasses where he had said they were. On my way out of the bedroom, I looked at the picture with the pendant draped across it. I thought, well in for a penny, in for a pound. So I carefully took the pendant off the picture frame, surely if this stubborn Irishman sees the two pendants together, it may convince him that this is his daughter.

I made my way downstairs, and I handed the glasses to Mr O'Conner. He said "Thank you, Oliver." He had remained standing, while Mrs Addison had sat down. Mr O'Conner put his glasses on, and said, "Mrs Addison, could I look at your pendant please?" She handed the pendant to him. He carefully looked at it, the back, then the front, especially the little red stones that were set in the shape of a Jesus cross. He then flicked it open to reveal the two photographs.

After a short time he looked up, and said, "Look Mrs Addison," still with anger in his voice "you are correct, that is me in the photograph, the other one is my daughter. I do not know where you have had this from, it does not belong to you. This is my daughter's. I do not know why you are under the illusion that you are my daughter. My daughter and my wife perished in a bombing raid in 1943. They found the remains of my wife and daughter, and the house was completely destroyed."

Mrs Addison stood up and looked at Mr O'Conner, she said very slowly, "Didn't you say your wife died in the bombing raid?" He replied, "Yes, she did." Then he said, "Look, this is very upsetting for me, would you please leave?" Mrs Addison had obviously seen the strong resemblance between herself and Mr O'Conner, also seemed in no doubt, she was in the presence of her father. Mrs Addison stood up, mom did the same. I looked at mom, she just smiled, she had guessed what I was up to. I thought this may be the last chance to maybe save the situation. After all I had promised Mrs Addison, I would try and make it possible for her to see the other pendant.

Will Mr O'Conner fly into a rage, when I bring the pendant from around from my back, where I had been hiding it, or would it jolt Mrs Addison's memory back into focus? I had to take that chance, so I said, "Mr O'Conner, please do not be angry with me, but I have brought the other pendant downstairs with me." The look he gave me, well, when I say the expression 'looked daggers at you', well, let's put it this way, there were lots of sharp pointy objects heading my way, courtesy of Mr. O'Connors glaring look, he snapped at me. "Ok, Oliver, as you have gone to the trouble of bringing it down, show it to Mrs Addison."

I did as he told me and handed it to her. She opened it and stared at the small photographs inside. She stared at them for a while, then wiped her eyes and stood up and said, "Alice, would you pass me my coat, please?" Mom said, "Yes, of course." As mom handed her coat to her, she said, "Ruth or you alright?" She answered, "I am fine, thank you."

She walked over to Mr O'Conner, who stood there holding a pendant in his left hand. She placed the other pendant in his right hand. She looked into his eyes. "Sorry to have troubled you, Mr O'Conner," and walked towards the front door. I noticed she had stopped. And was looking at what she would not realise I believe is the crayon drawing she did when she was a little girl. Mr O'Conner had hung it on the right-hand side of the front door, and it had certainly caught the attention of Mrs Addison. She stared at it for some time and finally opened the door.

She stood in the doorway and seemed to be hesitating. She then took a step back into the room. She once again stared at the picture. Mr O'Conner's father had done a really nice job of framing the drawing, putting glass in the front to protect the precious picture. Mrs Addison just stood there, then started to try drawing with her fingertips across the glass, as if drawing it again. Mom walked up to her and very gently put her hand on her shoulder. Mom said, "Ruth are you alright?"

She turned to mom and very quietly said, "Alice, my name is not Ruth." She hesitated, then looked past mom, looking directly to Mr O'Conner and said, "My real name is Sarah-Ann. My father always called me Saran. My name is Sarah-Ann O'Conner. My father is Shamus O'Conner the carpenter. My mother's name is Mary O'Conner, my wonderful mother."

By now she was sobbing uncontrollably. She walked up to Mr O'Conner who was now as white as a sheet and I could see his hands were visibly shaking. He was still holding the pendants. As she approached him, she said, "Hello my father I can remember it's a bit hazy but I remember that day and before."

Mr O'Conner just stood there motionless, mouth open. He closed his eyes and just said, "Oh dear god, it is really you, Sarah-Ann. She replied, "Yes, father, you know it's me, don't you?" "Yes, I know. The moment I saw the pendant and looked into your eyes I knew. I knew you're my little girl, well you are now, my big girl. Then he said, "Oliver, will you close the front door and will everybody please sit down? I think we have a lot to talk about."

Mom said, "Would you like us to leave you alone so you can talk?" They both said together, "No, no you must stay." "Ok," mom said. "I would just put the kettle on and make us a cup of tea." Mom and I went into the kitchen to give them a bit of privacy. The thing was we could hear every word they were saying. What I found amazing was Mr O'Conner never shed a single tear, but I saw the emotion in his face when she said, 'hello my father' but he was going to be the tough boxer soldier to the end, wasn't he? I heard her asking about her mother. He then began to explain what happened on that day. Then it went very quiet.

We then heard Mr O'Conner sobbing his heart out as the very painful memories would come flooding back. It is not nice to hear a woman crying but hearing a grown man crying brought tears to my eyes. Mom was already there with her head in her hands. Although I could not see mom's eyes, tears were dropping from the heel of her hands. Mr O'Conner must have composed himself as I could hear him continuing to explain what he knew of that day.

Then I heard her say, 'Dad, you know what happened to the Thorpe family and our neighbours." Mr O'Conner said, "Yes, Mr Thorpe died in France in world war two. Mrs Thorpe and her daughter died in the same bombing raids that your mom perished in." "Oh dear god, dad, I left her in the bedroom." "Sarah, whom did you leave?" "Elizabeth, Elizabeth Thorpe, my best friend. I left her in my bedroom. Mom had shouted up to me asking me to pop round to the shop which was in the next street to ours, if I would fetch some baking powder and some sweets for me and Elizabeth. I asked if she would like to come with me. She said she didn't as she did not feel well and it was raining anyway."

Mr. O'Conner said, "My dear daughter, what you have just told me has solved a mystery that has haunted me since that day. The fireman had told me they had found the remains of an adult female, and also they believed, a young female. That explains why they never found your pendant. That also explains why they only found the remains of Mrs. Thorpe but nothing of her daughter. But one of the neighbours had seen a young girl turning a corner at the top of the street, people automatically thought it was Elizabeth. They said her grandparents searched for her all night. They were told later she may have been picked up and taken with the other children when they evacuated them from the town. Sadly, they must have passed our house a few times in their search, where her remains lay, for them never to know. The Thorpes' house was also bombed as well. Yes, along with three others, the foundry, the steel factory, and of course the shop."

"Luckily dad, I remember stepping back into the middle of the roadway as I could hear the planes overhead. I was trying to get a better view of them. I think that saved my life. Dad! All those years lost, I only live a few miles from here, we may have passed in the street. Well, we cannot change the past, let's be grateful for now." Mr O'Conner said, "I agree, thanks to Oliver, we are together god bless him." "Dad, I have to tell you, you have two beautiful grandchildren and a son-in-law to meet."

Mom said, "Perhaps it's time to take the tea in." Mom had just picked up the tray, when we heard a loud thump, followed by a high-pitched scream. Mom dropped the tray with a crash, Mrs. Addison, was shouting, "Help!! Alice, Oliver come quick." We ran into the living room to be greeted by the sight of Mr. O'Conner lying on the floor with Mrs. Addison trying to turn him on his back, as he had gone face down. She was crying and shouting, "Dad, what is the matter?" We helped her turn him over. Once he was on his back we quickly realised we had to turn him onto his side as he was bleeding from his nose and mouth.

Mrs. Addison, said, "Quick, phone for an ambulance." Mom said, "I don't think Shamus has a phone." I said, "Mom, I think Jack next door has a phone." "Quick Oliver, go around and ask him." So I ran around and banged on Jack's door. Within a matter of seconds he opened the door. "What's happening Oliver? I thought I heard a scream." "I will explain in a minute but can you please phone for an ambulance?" I explained what had happened, and after he had phoned he said the hospital had told him the ambulance would be here in about ten minutes. Jack said, "I will come around next door with you and wait for the ambulance."

In a short time the ambulance arrived and took Mr. O'Conner to hospital. Mrs. Addison went with him. Which left me, mom and Jack to tidy up and make sure the house was locked up and secure. Earlier we had watched the ambulance disappear into the distance. I said to mom, "This is all my fault, isn't it?" Mom said that was a foolish thing to say. "You are a kind, thoughtful boy. There isn't any way that we could possibly know this was going to happen. I will ring later to find out how he is. Tomorrow we will go and visit him." This we did. Jack was there, so was Mrs Addison. Mr O'Conner was sitting up in bed and was quite cheerful. He looked at me and smiled. "Come here, Oliver." I approached him, he put his hand on top of my head and ruffled my hair. He then hugged me. Could this mean he has forgiven me?

"Your mom rang the hospital this morning. They allowed me to speak to her for a few minutes. She told me you feel guilty about what happened to me. Do not ever feel guilty. Quite the opposite. What you did for us, we can never repay you. Be incredibly proud of yourself. I said, "Are you sure?" "Oh, I am sure, Oliver," Mr O'Conner replied. I asked him about his injuries. "Oh, they are nothing. Flat nose and a cut lip. I had those before. Take me back to when I used to box." He just laughed, which made us all smile. I thought, tough man. "Thank god he is alright, mom." "Oliver, would you go and fetch us all a coffee or a cup of tea please?" Mom gave me the money and I set off down the long hallway. The machine was about halfway, I noticed someone was already at the machine.

I thought he seemed familiar. He was wearing a heavy black duffle type coat with a hood so the only thing I could see were his hands still. Something about him disturbed me. He quickly walked off down the hallway and I thought no more of it. I proceeded to get the drinks from the machine. I just happened to glance down the sloping hallway and standing at the bottom holding a drink and grinning his sickly grin, was Jake. My heart froze, what was he doing here? Then he pointed his finger at me and then ran his finger across his throat. There was no mistaking what he meant. He then disappeared around the corner. My mind was in a whirl. When I get back to the room do I tell everybody about who I have just seen?

Although unlikely, his being in the hospital could be quite innocent. He may be visiting his poor mother, probably put into hospital again by that cowardly bully of a father of his. Yes, that might be it. So I decided not to say anything. Perhaps it's for the best. As for Mr O'Conner, he certainly does not need any more stress at the moment. We said our goodbyes to Mr. O'Conner. When we reached the hospital car park Mrs Addison said the nurse had told her he would be home in a few days' time. She also told me he had a brain tumour and may have only six months to live, maybe more.

Looking at mom, she said, "Alice did you know?" Mom replied, "Yes, I am sorry, I was trying to find the right time to tell you. With what has gone on, it was impossible." "I understand. Alice, what am I going to do? I have just found him and in a matter of months, I could lose him." Mom put her arms around her. "We will have to make the most of what time he has left." "Yes, of course, Alice, you are right," Mrs. Addison said. "I will see you tomorrow." She got in her car and drove off. She had offered us a lift. But we decided to walk home.

We were chatting while we were walking and talked about the unbelievable experiences we had today. When I just happened to mention seeing Jake at the hospital. Mom stopped dead in her tracks. She grabbed my arm and pulled me back. She said, "Jake at the hospital?" "Yes, mom, I saw him in the corridor." Mom said, "Same corridor as Mr O'Conner's room is on?" "Oh dear, are you thinking what I'm thinking mom?" "Yes, we should make our way to Mr. O'Conner's house. About ten minutes later we arrived at Mr O'Conner's house.

There was a police car parked outside his house. We noticed Jack talking to a policeman, and we ran over to them. "Jack, what has happened?" Jack said, "You will not believe what has happened, someone has broken into Shamus' house and smashed almost everything in there. They have thrown red paint everywhere." Mom said to the policeman, "Have you any idea who it might be?" He replied, "At the moment, I can only make an educated guess."

The policeman looked towards the Garnetts' house. He did not have to say anything else. Mom asked the policeman if the neighbours had seen anybody or anything. The policeman said very angrily, "How could people not have seen anything or heard anything? You would think the houses opposite would have seen or heard something, they will not come forward anyway because of fear of retaliation." Jack asked if we could go into the house. The policeman replied, "Yes, but do not touch anything." The front door was almost off its hinges, the door frame was splintered where they must have jemmied the door.

Jack said, "Be careful. There is glass everywhere." We understood because all we could hear was glass crunching under our feet, after entering the house a short distance we were not prepared for the total destruction before our eyes. Mom had a sharp intake of breath, "Oh God!! they should burn in hell for doing this." Mom was in tears and said, "That poor man Shamus, his home is in ruins." What they had not smashed or ripped they had covered in bright red paint.

On the living room wall in bright red paint were the letters 'Go home, Paddy!!' "Mom, did you give Mrs Addison the two lockets when we were at the hospital?" "Yes, Oliver, I had picked them off the floor when Mr O'Conner had gone to the hospital. Looking at all this, it is a good job I did. I need to ask the policeman if he will notify Mrs Addison of what has happened here." The policeman said he would do that. Mom gave him her address. While they were talking, I sneaked back into the house.

I had noticed when we were leaving the house the drawing that had triggered Mrs. Addison's memory back. It was undamaged and I was not leaving without it. Thankfully, it was one of the few things that remained intact so I took it off the wall and hid it under my jacket. I had not realised how heavy and bulky it was. While mom was talking to the policeman. I noticed Jack was standing on his doorstep so I quietly walked over to Jack, and said to him, "This is very precious to Mr O'Conner." I asked him if he would keep it for now.

The following day after mom had finished her shift at the café, she caught the bus to the other side of town to go and see Mrs Addison, to see how she was coping after this distressing news about her father's house. I had not seen Mrs. Addison at school that day. I told Milly what had happened over the last few days on our way home from school, we had to pass Mr O'Conner's house. They had boarded up the windows and the doorway. I wondered what was going to happen to his belongings and those beautiful paintings that we never got to see. Walking down the alleyway we came level with the Garnetts' house. The Garnetts' garden wall was this grubby white?

For safety, we stood at the corner with our backs against the wall. We bravely waited and listened. Getting ready to run if we need to. But it was quiet and no attack, thank god. Milly with a serious look on his face and hands on hips said, "Olly, we have to do something. Let's get our revenge on them for what they have done." "That's ok Milly, but how? They are bigger and stronger than we are." I could see the cogs in Milly's brain working. "So, we are going to need some beer bottles." "That's no good. Are you crazy?" "No, it's not to drink. It's a firebomb." "Yeah!!" I said, "do you know how to make one, Milly?" "No, but I know they use a bottle and put something in the bottle. Then light it and throw it." "Forget that, Milly, I think we would do more harm to ourselves than anybody else."

Still, Milly wasn't to be put off. His next idea was even crazier, fire arrows. He said he would shoot fire arrows over the wall he was serious about this and practised firing arrows over the Garnetts' wall. Milly the archer, with pretend arrows, there was the sound of chuff, chuff, yeah. That just doubled me up with laughter, Milly turned around and saw me laughing, he shouted, "Oliver, this is serious." I wiped the tears from my eyes. Then Milly saw the funny side of it and started laughing. Milly said, "I suppose it is a bit crazy." I replied, "It's a lot crazy, but I know where you're coming from. Where the hell would we get a bow from? And who would supply us with flaming arrows?" Milly said, "The flaming arrow and bow shop." We both howled with laughter.

Milly said, "Shush, they might hear us." We stopped and listened. We could hear some kids playing in the background. And the drone of cars from the roadway. But nothing else. I looked at Milly and shrugged my shoulders. "Let's go." Milly grabbed my arm and said, "Wait." I looked into those big black eyes through those ridiculous spectacles he wears. I knew his brain cogs were turning again. I groaned because I knew there was another cunning Milly plan again. "Hey, Olly, how about catapults?" "Yes, Milly, what about catapults?"

Me and mom love Milly so much as he is one of the kindest and most comical of all people I know. And I love him to bits in a manly way, of course. I know I can trust him with my life and vice versa. But he can be quite annoying sometimes. Once he gets a bee in his bonnet, there is no stopping him. So, I thought I had better humour him else he will not shut up. Milly said, "Catapults, Olly." "Yes, but remember we were banned from having them." "But we bought them anyway. If you remember we have the ones with the extra strong elastic for more power." "Yes, I remember now, Mill, didn't you hide them in your dad's shed?" "Yes. If we knew how far away the Garnetts' house was we could work out the trajectory and we could break all their windows . There are thousands of stones here in the alleyway. We can use those as ammunition."

I put my hands on Milly's shoulders and looked him in the eye and said "Milly, my little friend, won't they know that it's us?" "No, of course not," Milly replied. I could see that I wasn't going to convince him not to do this. So I said, "Ok, Milly. How do we do this?" I watched as he ran over to the Garnetts' wall. I saw him look up to the top of the wall. Probably working out the height. I was leaning on the opposite wall with my arms folded. Being amused just watching Milly, Trying to figure out what he was going to do next.

The alleyway is quite wide so I was about twenty feet from Milly. After what happened to me in this alleyway, I was quite reluctant to go anywhere near the Garnetts' wall. The wall was rounded at the top making it impossible to climb up, even if you could jump that high. Milly said, "If I stood on your shoulders, I could see over the wall."I started to make my way over to him. I noticed Milly had turned to face the wall once more. Probably working out his plan of attack. I was about halfway across the alleyway when Milly let out this awful scream. He rapidly started to back away from the wall and took to his heels. I have never seen him run so fast. He had this dust cloud following him as the alleyway was basically a dirt track.

It is now July and very hot. I could hear Milly still screaming. He shouted to me, "Run, Oliver, run." I just froze on the spot. I expected the Garnetts' heavy garden gate to fly open and be confronted by Jake the snake. To my great relief, the garden gate stayed shut. I could still hear Milly shouting. I needed to get to him. And find out what had frightened him so much. I got my legs moving again and ran down the alleyway. I found Milly behind some bins. He was crying and I said, "Milly, what the hell happened?" With a shaky voice he said, "It's him." "Who Milly? Who did you see?" "Jake It was Jake." "Where Milly, I did not see him."

He was now screaming again, his eyes were full of fear. He kept repeating, "The wall, the wall." I said, "What about the wall? His face, Oliver. It was on the wall." I said, "Calm down and tell me exactly what happened." I crouched down beside Milly and put my arm around him. I could feel him shaking. "Ok, Milly, tell me everything about it." "You know when I turned to you and said about climbing on your shoulders? Well, when I turned back around. There it was his grinning evil face. But the worst part, Oliver was when he jumped out of the wall and came at me. Oliver, I did not imagine this. I swear on my mom's life. It was real. You know, I would not say that unless I really believed what I had seen." "I am sorry Milly, I did not see or hear anything. I just heard your frightening scream. It made the hairs stand up on the back of my neck. I knew something had really frightened you. Because the next thing I saw was you running like a greyhound. Never seen you move so fast." I know Milly is not the sort of person to imagine things. So as crazy as it might sound, I believed him. I said, "Come on Milly, I will take you to my house." Believe me, we did not walk, we ran all the way.

I don't think mom is back from visiting Mrs Addison, I put the key in the lock, but before I could enter Milly ran past me, shouting, "Let me in, let me in." Once we were inside, Milly seemed to calm down a bit. I said, "Mill, do you want to eat or drink anything?" "Not now, thank you," he replied. Just then, the front door opened. Mom was back I explained to mom how frightened Milly was. Mom said to Milly, "Come on. We will take you home and explain to your mother what has happened. Rueben Millhouse, you will be ok." Mom put her hand to her forehead and said, "God, what next?" Milly's mom thanked us for bringing him home. Before we left I said, "Mill, see you tomorrow." "Ok, Oliver, I'll see you at school. I am not going down that alleyway ever again." "Ok, Mill. I will meet you at your house tomorrow and we'll go to school together. A different way." "Thank you, Oliver."

On our way back home, mom said, "Do you think Rueben really saw anything?" "I don't know, mom, but it scared the pants off Milly, whatever it was." When we were back home mom said, "Sit down, I have something to tell you. Mr O'Conner is coming out of hospital tomorrow and will be staying at his daughter's house. Just for now. Perhaps things have worked out for the best as he is with somebody that will look after him and care for him. They have sent somebody to collect all his belongings and his paintings. Jack said he would help to sort things out for him."

Mom said on her way back from the market she had decided to get something for our tea. She had bumped into Mrs Garnett, and asked her how things were. "She knew what I meant. She smiled and said, "a bit better." At least as far as I could see, she did not seem to be suffering any injuries and no black eyes which made a change for the poor woman. I asked if she had been in the hospital recently. She shook her head and said, "No. Why do you ask?" So I said, "The reason I ask is because Oliver had told me he saw Jake in the hospital corridor." She said, "Did this happen when Mr O'Conner was in the hospital?" I said yes, it was. She looked to the floor as if absorbing what I had just told her.

When she finally looked up, her eyes were wide. More, I think, with anger than anything else. She had put two and two together and come up with Jake. I could see she was very angry. She virtually spat out the words, "Evil, evil boy." After a short time, she seemed calm. She said, "I'm so sorry. I do not think anybody could understand what my life is really like. She told me that Jake was not her natural son and she had adopted him when her only sister died in childbirth and that Gary was her own son. And there was about a two year difference between them, Jake being the elder. I asked why Jake's father didn't look after him. She said his birth certificate had stated 'father unknown'. "We tried to trace him, but it was hopeless. Nobody seems to know who he was." Her friend said they sometimes saw her sister with this tall, dark man. She never actually met him as after her sister Sharon had started her relationship with him, they barely saw her at all. And being the only close relative left in the family as their parents had died a few years earlier, she had felt it her duty and for the sake of her sister to take the boy on.

She said, "Alice, it was the biggest mistake of my life. I cannot see or find any resemblance to my lovely, kind hearted sister. Only what appears to be the traits of the father and he probably was as spiteful and evil as his offspring."

She then said something that shocked me. "Did you know that when I first met Reggie Garnett, he was the kindest, most gentle man you could ever wish to meet? People ask me now, why do I stay with him? And I tell them because I can still see that kind gentle man I fell in love with, and I know one day he will return to me. When we were first married Reg had a job as a lorry driver. Although he had nights away the money was good and he loved the job. The money he was earning, including the money he saved by sleeping in his cab instead of a nice warm comfortable bed, enabled us to have a nice home around us. So, you see he is not the person you see today."

I asked her what she thought might have changed him so much. She said, "Well, everything seemed perfect. We had a nice home and Reg had a good job. We had adopted Jake. Jake was his registered name and it was Reg who insisted we give him that name, but I started to notice slight changes in Reggie's behaviour. He had started being late for work, eventually he stopped going to work altogether and they sacked him. He started drinking and smoking, which he had never done before. When I questioned him why he was behaving like he was, that's when the violence started. Next we had police on our doorstep every five minutes and they knew it was somebody in the family. They knew Jake was up to no good, but the police never seemed to be able to charge him anything. He seemed to have a charmed life where crime was concerned. He seemed to be able to do just what he wanted. I thought when Gary was born it would change Reg. But he showed no interest in us at all. He was all Jake. I have suffered this for a long time, too long."

She then said, "I will have to go now, Alice." So, I said "Thank you for talking to me, Christine. You have made things a lot clearer in my mind now. I hope things get better for you." As she walked away, she replied, "I doubt it. But thank you anyway." She suddenly stopped and turned to me.

She smiled and said, "Have a guess whose sixteenth birthday was yesterday?" I just shook my head and shrugged my shoulders. "Who?" Just work it out Alice my friend. You will understand." With that, she disappeared into the crowded marketplace. "Oliver, you've always said that when you were anywhere near Jake, you always sensed an order of evil about him. Oliver dear, your senses may prove right."

I have got back to normal, as normal as can be anyway. Mom was still working as hard as ever. When I'm on my own, I start to think what life might have been like if I had a father. What sort of father abandons his wife? Perhaps we are better off without him. Mrs Addison has had permission from the school to do a three-day week so that she can help look after her father. Luckily her husband works from home, so that helps.

We think the Garnetts are up to their old tricks again. There was a local warehouse broken into. Thousands of pounds worth of goods were stolen. Nobody saw anything. No fingerprints, absolutely nothing, the Garnetts always seemed to have alibis. I had heard the police had been watching the Garnetts' house on and off for years, but the burglary continued even while they were watching the house. The police had said it was like trying to catch ghosts.

It is Saturday today and I am just off round to Milly's. I fancied a game of football down the park but I don't think Milly is too keen on football or any sport, come to think of it. He likes playing chess or draughts. He likes to keep that super-duper brain exercised. When I asked him why he preferred playing chess instead of sport, you know, keeping fit. His reply was, "The only thing I might get from playing chess is a headache, your so-called sport people seem to get broken legs and arms and whatever else," with his nose in the air.

He said, "No thanks you can stick to your sports. The last time I played football with you, you put me in goal because your friends said I don't know how to kick a ball. So there I was in the goal and that big lad called Tanky or something who was playing for the other side kicked the ball so hard I landed in the back of the net. I could not breathe properly for the week after that." "Ok, Mill, what do you want to do?" He said, "Let's go down to the stream by the railway. We can try and catch some sticklebacks. I think mom has got some empty jars and I have got a couple of fishing nets." I heard Mill shouting to his mom could he have the two empty jam jars off the window sill? I heard his mom reply, "Ok but just be careful."

We made our way across large pieces of wasteland to get to the stream. It was a kids' paradise. There was long grass, perfect for playing cowboys and Indians. There were lots of trees we could climb. Somebody had dumped a couple of old cars, but the best was an old lorry and an abandoned rusty old crane which me and Milly loved. We had a pretend drive of the lorry but when we reached the crane, which was perched on top of this dirt hill, there were about five of these small dirt hills, perfect for kids with bikes which we didn't have yet. We decided to give the crane a miss because there were about half a dozen kids playing on it.

It was another lovely hot day. Lots of flies about, lots of bumble bees whizzing about. Occasional wasp. I hate them. They just sting you for the sake of it. Farther on we came to this large pool. Which mom told me to keep away from but being boys, we decided to walk around the edge of the pool. The pool is surrounded by trees and bushes. I had heard somebody say the pool was bottomless and was very dangerous.

We had walked about halfway round the pool when this boy came running towards us screaming his head off. He was wearing a blue button up shirt which was open and flapping behind him. His two friends were behind him flailing their arms about and shouting. He came up to us and said, "My back, have a look at my back." We just stood there. He said, "My back is really hurting." His friends caught up with him. One of his friends lifted his shirt up and looked at his back and saw it was covered in wasps merrily stinging away. I said, "Quick, take off your shirt." As he did, they started to swarm around us, Milly just ran, flapping his arms about, proving again who has the brains. I took the boy's shirt and started swatting them off his red and very lumpy back. Then I felt a sting on my neck. 'Ow well, that was enough for me. I was off catching up with Milly.

We eventually reached our destination. We had to approach the stream by walking along a road by that ran parallel with the stream, (someone had fenced off the stream), we found a gap under part of the fence when we reached the gap. We looked around. It was clear so Milly squeezed under first.

I followed straight after him. The only problem is, the embankment down to the stream is quite steep and consists of gravel and dirt. We had to slide down on our bottoms. We got down without breaking our jars. First thing I did was to wet my handkerchief from the stream and put it on my neck where the wasp had stung me. At first it made it worse, me and Mill sat down on the bank with our fishing nets and jars ready. There were trees and bushes lining the bank on the other side of the stream.

There was a huge willow tree a bit farther down which created shade over the water so we could see these sticklebacks easier. Mill was already there, with his fishing net fishing away. He is determined to beat me as chief stickleback catcher. "Come on, Oliver, down here you can see the fish better." But I was too comfortable where I was, with the warm sunshine on my back. The air was so still there was no wind at all, the only sounds were the trickling of the stream as it passed by and the fluttering and singing of the birds in the trees. The sun glittering on the water made me squint my eyes.

It was so peaceful I forgot about stickleback fishing. But little did I know that in the future these moments of peace would be few and far between. I heard a car pass by on the road above, then it was quiet. I looked up into the bright blue sky. Not a single cloud anywhere. Well, I suppose I had better get fishing or I will never hear the last of it. I was just about to move when something cast a dark shadow over me. A big shadow as it stretched over the stream and onto the other bank. I thought it was a cloud blocking the sun. It couldn't be as there were no clouds in the sky at all.

But before I could turn to see what it was, it disappeared, leaving us with bright sunshine once more. That really was weird, so I ran along the bank to Milly for a bit of Milly protection. He might be small and mouse-like at times he can appear to be quite timid but you get him going he's like a ferret up a drainpipe. In other words, he can be quite vicious. Because in the next few minutes I was going to need him to be just that vicious. I heard behind me, footsteps and the words, "What you doing, nerds?

Those words sent shivers down my back. For the second I thought Jake had found us, but as I turned there were three boys. They looked about our age. One of the boys who was quite stocky had a large mop of unruly blonde hair and had a round, not unkindly face which was covered in freckles. I looked at the boy standing at the back and had to do a double take because he looked identical to the boy I just looked at. Obviously twins. The one twin said, "Do you know that there are leeches in that stream? Me and Milly looked at each other and started to laugh. Now the last time I laughed at somebody, I got a flattened nose. At least they were on the other side of a six foot fence. Which I think gave Milly, a bit of Dutch courage. The next words I heard came from Milly's mouth.

With his tough guy stance, hands on his hips he delivered the sarcastic words: "Suppose you're going to tell us there are crocodiles in there next." Then Milly stuck his tongue out at them and blew a few raspberries. Big mistake because the boy standing closest to the fence, the one with the black curly hair and big teeth, became very angry and said, "Let's get him." He started shaking the fence as if expecting it to fall down. My stomach did a flip. I realised one of the twins had started to walk towards the gap in the fence we had climbed through.

Then I heard a shout here. "We can get through here." I turned to Milly to tell him to run. But he was already halfway across the stream, whether there were leeches or crocodiles in the stream, it wasn't going to stop Milly. He might not be vicious at the moment. But certainly being a ferret boy, can he move when he wants to. Luckily, the stream is only about two feet deep and is only about 6 feet across but was agonisingly slow going. Milly stood on the bank I was heading for, waiting there with his arms outstretched to help me up the slippery bank. He was also watching what those boys were doing, I can tell you there was sheer panic on his face." He said, "Quick Oliver, they are coming." That spurred me on and with the help of Milly I was up the bank like a shot.

We weaved our way through the bushes and trees that lined the bank of the stream. After a short time we managed to get clear of the trees. Only to be confronted by what looked like a huge field of either corn or wheat. The farmer who owned the field was not going to be very happy but we had no choice. We just ran headlong into the field of whatever it was. I'm sure the farmer would tell us what crop it is if he catches us.

While still moving, I said to Milly, "I think it would be better if we split up. It should confuse them. They didn't appear to be too intelligent." "I think we had better keep moving fast." "Ok, Mill, I'll go left, you go right." I could hear them coming behind us. All of a sudden I heard a scream. I thought they've caught Milly so I stopped and listened. Then I heard a sound like something crashing through the foliage and through the trees, I heard a loud splash. Something or someone had landed in the stream by the sounds of it.

I was just about to shout, "Milly!" When another scream rang out. The same thing. Something crashing through the trees again, this time accompanied by the sound of branches snapping. Closely followed by a splash again. Then this happened for the third time. We could hear the hell of a commotion on the other side of the trees, I could hear shouting. Then I clearly heard somebody shout. "Get out, get out, it's a ghost." Then I heard Milly's voice shouting, "Oliver, Oliver, are you alright?" So I shouted back, "I'm ok, Mill. Can you make your way back over to me?" After about five minutes Mill managed to find me. I said to Mill, "I can't hear anything, shall we go back to the stream to see what has happened?" Mill replied, "No it might be a trap." "Mill, what do you think we should do?" "Well, if we carry on up the field, we could meet a very angry farmer with a shotgun. So I don't think we want that." I thought, 'Oh god, what have I done by asking Milly what we should do? We could be here till midnight'. He has to analyse everything.

He suddenly said, "I have it. I have a very cunning plan. We won't go forwards or backwards, thus eliminating any chance of meeting any enemies." I groaned again, "Is that your plan, Mill?" "Yes, Oliver we go left." I groaned again. "So that's your cunning plan? We just go left?" "Yes, Oliver, stop sneering. By going to the edge of the field, then going roughly at a 45° angle we should get to the bend in the stream. There's a bridge there and we can get back onto the main road." "Sorry, I sneered, Mill sounds good. Let's go."

Like Mill said, the bridge was exactly where he said it would be. We crossed the bridge onto the main road, this is a roadway that takes you into the town centre and can be very busy at times. But today seemed fairly quiet, there was a small amount of traffic. A few people were walking on the other side of the road. We started to make our way back home. We had only walked a few yards when Mill said, "Look Oliver." There were wet footprints on the pavement.

We followed the footprints and spotted a figure leaning against a garden wall. Along this roadway there are big posh houses and this figure did not look as if he belonged there. As he looked quite dishevelled we had already guessed who it was. So for safety reasons we crossed over to the other side of the road.

As we drew level with the figure we realised it was the bigger boy with the dark curly hair. His back was against the wall. He was leaning forward with his hands on his knees. His shirt was badly torn, he was soaking wet and I'm sure in between the noise of the traffic I could hear him crying. I said to Mill, "You stay here. I have to find out what has happened." So I crossed the road. I very carefully approached him. I was right. He was crying. There were cuts and scratches on his hands.

I very quietly asked him if he was alright. His head shot up, he went rigid and said, "What? What?" His eyes were wide with fear. I said, "It's ok mate, we just wanted to know what happened to you and your friends." "We were chasing you in that cornfield when something grabbed me by my ankle. The next thing I knew, I was flying through the air and I crashed through the trees landing in the stream, exactly the same happened to the twins. All of us were grabbed by the ankle and thrown through the trees, ending up in the stream. I was lucky. Alan, one of the twins, broke his arm. His brother had a bad gash on his forehead. We had to drag Alan through the hole in the fence, he was screaming his head off. At first I thought I had put my foot in one of those bear traps you see in films. That is exactly what it felt like, I still have the marks on my ankle."

He pulled his jeans' leg up and showed me. There were strange rows of indentations. They ran in two rows across the outside of his right ankle. There were about four or five indentations in each row, each indentation was about half inch square. On the inside rows were eight or nine inches apart. But much smaller and went all the way round the inside of his ankle. There is nothing that I can think of that could possibly have made those marks. This boy was really shaken up by what had happened to him.

We were lucky that whatever got to them did not get to us as well. I said to him, "My friend says he is sorry for taking the mick." He said, "That's ok we would have probably turned him upside down and just shook him. I said no hard feelings then. He replied, no, no hard feelings. "Your ankle looks swollen, does it hurt?" "Oh yeah. It's killing me. I am waiting for the pain to ease. Then I'm going home. God knows what mom and dad are going to say when they see the state I am in." "You know, for somebody who we thought was just another bully, he turned out not to be too bad a person." He asked me if I thought maybe the farmer had set a special trap for trespassers. I said, "Wow! That would be some trap if he had."

But what baffled me is whatever it was that attacked them, gripped them with just enough force as not to do too much damage. It then threw them with great accuracy through the trees and as far as I could tell they all landed in the stream. I asked him his name. He said, "Dave, my name is Dave." "I'm Oliver and my friend over there is Milly." He looked over to Milly, raised his hand, waved and shouted. "Hi Reuben!" Milly gave a very wobbly wave back. Dave said to Oliver, "I have to go." He groaned as he pushed himself off the wall, he said, see you around Olly, he turned around and smiled, then turned back and limped away.

I then joined Milly on the other side of the road. I said, "Mill, I think we had better get back home before anything weird happens." I might not have mentioned this, but the name of our town is Wychwood, which is spelled the old English way. It is in the county of Wisham. At the moment our town seems to be living up to its name of wychwood. Some say the name of the town came from the witch hazel trees that were in abundance here. Others say it's because witches used to dance around their cauldrons casting spells in the woods.

Eventually we got home and we were both really tired. That night, as soon as my head hit the pillow, I drifted off into a deep sleep, only to have my old night nightmare return. I seem to be in exactly the same place, the same cliffs, waterfall, stream, moonlight - everything appeared to be the same but I felt different. I felt bigger, somehow I was bigger. No, I wasn't just bigger. I was huge. Massive. I even towered over some of the pine trees to my right. I felt powerful, invincible.

I looked at my feet, they were enormous like the rest of me. One blessing, my pyjamas seemed to have grown with me. I looked around, no sign of the little China man, no sign of his big ugly friend either, but like in the repeated nightmare I had before, there is only one direction I can go, that is forward. So, I thought, head for the stream and hope I will wake up soon.

I started to make my way down the grassy slope towards the stream. I took about four or five steps. I noticed the ground was shaking. I thought, Oh no, not him again, thinking it was the creature, but the ground had stopped shaking. Get a grip, Oliver, it's you that's causing the ground to shake. That made me chuckle. But why this time? Am I a giant? Why am I surprised? These nightmares do not make any sense at all. Me, a giant making the ground shake! I reached the stream. I waited and listened. Nothing happened. Then I remembered it was only when I crossed the stream that things started to happen. I hesitated, not knowing what to expect.

Would that man with long hair appear? Or would little and large come onto the scene again? With his little dragon flying around. I hope they do because they are going to get a big shock when they see giant Oliver instead of little Oliver. So, I stepped across the stream in one stride, ha! In one stride! Great, I thought, right, I am going to find out what is on the other side of that hill. Perhaps find the man with the long hair, but before I could take another step, I could feel the ground shaking again. Well, it was not me this time as I was standing completely still.

Then I saw the top of the China man's head suddenly appear on the brow of the hill followed seconds later by the massive head of his creature friend. They continued to walk towards me, the Chinese man had not seen me as he had his head down, looking at something in his left hand, but his creature friend had certainly seen me. It was only when the creature made the strange sound of arrrgh' when the China man decided to look up. When he saw me, not believing his eyes, he slowly went from my feet to my head. The look on his face, I will treasure.

These were two beings, three if you count the little dragon that were hunting me down. Why, it is still a mystery to me. I shouted at the little China man, I think more in anger than anything else. These nightmares have disrupted my life long enough. I want answers. My voice boomed out. Why? If the Chinese man had hair I'm sure it would have stood on end. My voice echoed off the cliff walls, making it sound even louder. The Chinese man's saucer eyes appeared to go back to normal. He seemed to have regained his composure then through gritted teeth he uttered the word "attack." I raised my clenched fists in front of me, anticipating that the creature would do his master's bidding but the creature did not move.

Beth

It just stood there making that odd sound of 'arrrgh again. I looked over at the Chinese man and said, "What are you going to do now?" Mr Chinese man, he struck his staff down hard against the ground, making the dragon on top of his staff flap its wings. The Chinese man pointed towards me with his extremely long, curved fingernails. If mom had been here she would have said, "With nails like that how could he do any work? And how could he possibly wipe his bottom?"

The thought made me smile which annoyed Mr China man even more. Still pointing at me, he gave the command strike to his tiny dragon. It flew straight at my face, claws and teeth bared at me. This was just a fly that needed swatting, so I did just that. As it approached me, I swung my massive right hand. I felt it connect and it made this sort of loud smacking sound. I watched as it spun out of control before disappearing a good distance away into the treetops. I immediately felt guilty about swatting that poor little dragon. I could have killed it. I hope not. I have never killed anything in my life. What am I thinking about?

As real as this dream appears to be, it's a dream, Oliver. Nothing dies in a dream, or does it? Well, I had the odd couple to sort out, but before I could say or do anything The Chinese man said, "Run, you useless lump. Run." With that, they disappeared over the hill. Then I heard a voice from the other side of the hill. "You will regret this." I heard a very shrill whistle. My attention was drawn to rustling in the pine trees, I saw the little dragon fly out from the top of the trees. At least I had not killed it. As it flew across towards the hilltop, it turned its head to stare at me, its red eyes glowing.

It disappeared over the hill then there was absolute silence. I thought, I have to see what is over that hill. So I made my way to the top. Standing on the top, I tried to take in the landscape that stretched out in front of me. Well, I was disappointed because all I could see was forest after forest of pine trees, valleys and snow-capped mountains in the distance. There was no sign of my enemies. I don't really know what I was expecting to see. I looked to my left. Because I was quite high up I had a good view of the top of the pine trees. About fifty yards in from the edge of the trees, I noticed a circle of trees that were flat and seemed to cover quite a large area, then just three small circles. They resembled the crop circles I have seen in the news on the tv, so I thought I would have to have a look.

Then I woke up. Damn it. "Sorry mom, did you hear my voice from across the landing?" She said, "Yes, go to sleep." It is now mid-September and for the last couple of weeks, it has done nothing except rain, but looking out of the window, it looks like today is nice and sunny. For some reason, I feel it's going to be a special day today. I went to see Mr.O'Conner the other day but it was not looking good as he is now in a wheelchair, but he still appears to be quite cheerful. Mrs Addison seems to be coping ok. She told me she had asked the local art gallery if she could display her father's paintings. They agreed and also invited her to display her paintings alongside her father's. She was absolutely over the moon about that. Some other good news is we haven't seen the hide nor hair of the Garnetts, although I have heard they are still up to their usual criminal activities. Surely one day. Still, they are leaving us alone.

Well, I have just had my breakfast and I am ready for school. Mom came downstairs and said, "Teeth, Oliver, have you cleaned your teeth?" "Oh no mom, I will go and clean them now." I quickly ran upstairs to the bathroom. While I was scrubbing my teeth, I thought I heard a knock at the door. Mom shouted up, "Oliver, did you ask Rueben to meet you here?" "No mom, I didn't," Mom replied, "Well, he is here waiting at the door for you."

I thought that's strange. Since we had stopped going down the alleyway to school I had been meeting him at his house. This is odd, I think my little friend Milly is up to something. I came downstairs and mom had left the front door open. I could see Milly standing at the front gate. He had his back to me. I shouted, "Be with you in a minute, Mill." Without turning around, he shouted back, "Ok." I noticed he was looking to his right and was on tiptoe. What the hell is he up to? The lady who owns the cafe where mom works, Mrs Coyne, had told mom that she didn't like the thought of me and mom having to carry all those cakes to the cafe, so she now picks up mom and her cakes, which means I don't have to get up so early.

The van had just arrived. I noticed on the side of the van, it had the name Coyne's café with pictures of meals they did, and mom's cakes and apple pie. I shouted, "Mrs Coyne's here for you, mom." Mom replied, "Ok, Oliver, on my way." So, I thought, right, let's just see what Milly is up to. Well, we have a short pathway to the front gate, which Milly was leaning on. So I crept up behind him and in a very loud voice said, "Whatcha doin' Mill?" He nearly jumped out of his skin. He quite angrily said, "Christ, Oliver, I wish you would not do that. I looked into those big glasses of his and said, "Milly, you are up to something. What is it?" He very sheepishly said, "Nothing, Oliver." "Honest, ok then, Mill, do you really want to go through the alleyway, especially after what happened to you?" Milly replied, "No, no, no, never. Let me get this straight. We are not going left, we're going right today, which happens to be the longest way round to school." Ok, Mill, you're the brains of the outfit I'll just follow you."

For ten minutes or so now I keep hearing what sounds like a garden gate opening and closing. I could hear a rusty squeak of gate hinges, then a bang as the latch on the gate would hit the gatepost. Probably some young kids who have moved into Mrs Steen's house two doors down, while I was saying bye to mom and closing our gate. I noticed Milly had disappeared. Then I spied him standing by what used to be Mrs Steen's front garden gate? The lady, mom had said she wasn't a very nice person, but we still went to a funeral to pay our respects, and I know mom was right in doing so, because mom had found out her husband was killed in the first world war, and then lost her only son in the second world war, anybody would be grumpy and sad after that?

Anyway, I am off to see what Milly is up to. He appeared to be talking to someone and as I approached Milly, it all became clear. I understood why he wanted to go the long way to school. He was talking to a girl and not just an ordinary girl. Wow! She just simply took my breath away. I was about ten feet away from them. I could not move. I was mesmerised by this stunningly beautiful creature in front of me and I am definitely not talking about Milly. I had asked mom when did she know she had fallen in love with my dad, and how do you know when you have fallen in love? What does it feel like? Mom said you will know when you are in love. When you meet that special person, your soulmate. She said it may be different from person to person. You might even hear angels singing, well I think they're having a party in my stomach at the moment.

Me and Mill have had quite a few girlfriends and one in particular, I really did like, but the feelings I am having for this girl that I have not even met yet, goes far beyond just liking. I think I may be in love. 'Don't be stupid, Oliver. You're too young to fall in love. But I am telling you, Brain, I am sure I am in love.' Brain to Oliver, 'have you asked your heart what he thinks?' Yes, heart says, definitely love'. I have to meet and talk to her, I am sure if she speaks to me I will turn into this shaking, babbling wreck, and speaking in tongues not known to man. I have to get away from here. Speak to her when I am looking cooler. Yeah, t-shirt and jeans. I look good in a t-shirt and jeans. And rehearse what I am going to say to her. Knock her dead with some cool phrases. What cool phrases, Oliver? You don't know any ok, retreat. Oh no too late, she just looked at me. She turned to Rueben and in a voice that sounded very much like angels singing (it was just like mom had said), she said, "Who is your friend, Rueben?"

Mill turned to me and said, "Oh, this is Oliver, my best friend." She said, "Hello, Oliver." With a very feeble wave of my hand, I said, "Hello." Then Mill with a wave of his hand said, "Come on over here and meet Beth." Beth, oh god, her name is as beautiful as she is. Right Oliver, your dream girl is about ten feet away. Move, brain to legs, walk. Oh no. Legs on strike. Now, now, I am moving. I will be next to her any moment now. Then disaster. I tripped on the edge of a raised paving slab. I stumbled forward, desperately trying to regain my balance and my pride, only to land with both hands on the gate that Beth was holding.

After a few seconds I realised I was a few inches away from Beth's face and I was looking into the most beautiful big green eyes I have ever seen. I said, "Sorry." I hadn't realised one of my hands was on top of hers. I removed my hand, very reluctantly, I might add, repeating how sorry I was. She said,

"That's ok, Oliver. No harm done." And then in my left ear, I heard a little chuckling voice saying, 'enjoy your trip, Oliver'. I could strangle him. Perhaps later. Surprisingly, I expected her to move away from me, but she more or less stayed where she was. I think she was saying something to me because those beautiful pouting lips of hers were moving.

She was speaking words my brain did not recognise, then I felt a sharp jab in my ribs. It was Milly's elbow. I heard Milly's voice. "Oliver", Beth was saying to you, 'do you live at no 23?' Beth had her hand over her mouth and was chuckling to herself. I thought to myself, Oliver, you have blown it. She probably thinks you are a clumsy fool. Even Milly was laughing at me. Double strangling later. Pride well and truly dented. I regained my composure and stood as straight and tall as I could and said 'Beth, I am sorry, but the trip seems to have got me a bit confused. Yes I do live at 23" She looked at Milly, then both of them just burst into hysterical laughter.

I said, "Ok, what's funny?" Milly, when he managed to catch his breath, just said, "Did you enjoy your trip Oliver?" Then I saw the funny side of it and started laughing with them. The next thing I know Beth's mom suddenly opened their front door and shouted, "Beth Come on, you'll be late for school." Beth's mom looked over to us and said, "Hello boys." Beth's mom seemed nice. Beth said, "Got to go." With that, she turned around. Her beautiful golden hair swirled as she turned and quickly disappeared into her house.

Me and Mill started to walk, getting ready to start running or else we were going to be late for school. As we were walking, I turned to Mill and said, "You sly dog, you. That's why you wanted to come this way. How did you know she lived there?" Milly said, "I was out with mom the other day, and mom bumped into this woman she used to go to school with. It just happened to be Beth's mom. Beth was with her at the time and I got talking to her. She told me they had moved into 27 Victoria street just yesterday, a few doors away from you, Beth's mom was born in Wychwood but when she got married they moved down south.

Beth's dad became very ill and they lost everything, but out of the blue the lady who lived at 27 left her house to them in her will. They are completely baffled as to why she would do that Oliver." Mill said, with a dreamy look on his face, "Oliver, I think she is absolutely gorgeous. I am in love." "Mill, don't be stupid. We had better get running. We're going to be late for school."

Then a voice from behind made us whirl around as we realised the voice belonged to Beth. She said, "Wait for me. I have to go the same way as you." She caught up with us, running at quite a fast pace. She flew past us shouting, "Come on." God, she is an athlete as well. We managed to catch up with her. I joined her on her right, Mill on her left. I noticed Mill kept dropping back. I wonder why? We eventually reached the main road. I guessed Beth would be going to the girls' school and would have to go to the right. We have to go to the left. Without breaking stride, she swung right and said 'bye. We said 'bye, and watched her disappearing down the road. I said to Mill, absolute "Poetry in motion." Mill replied with an open mouth, "Yeah." Obviously, we were late for school but it was worth it.

I met Mill after school and it was obvious which route he wanted to take. While we were walking back home, Mill said, "Do you think she will be there at her gate again?" I said, "Mill, I don't know." Mill said, "If she is there, would you do me a favour?" Not really thinking about it, I said, "Yes, of course, Mill." "Oliver, promise." "Ok, Mill, I promise." He then handed me an envelope. I narrowed my eyes at him and said, "Mill, what the heck is this?" Mill replied, "It's for Beth. I want you to give it to Beth. Please, you promised." "Ok, Mill. I did promise." As we were about 200 yards from Beth's house we could hear a garden gate repeatedly going squeak, bang, squeak, bang. Utterly childish and juvenile but we didn't care.

In fact, I found it very endearing. She was a free spirit but I am sure some of the neighbours could find it quite irritating though. Suddenly, Mill broke into a run and half turning to me said, "See you at the top of the street." In the same breath he said, "Do not forget the letter." I waved him on and said, "Ok." As I approached Beth's house, she had stopped swinging on the gate, and was now casually hanging over it, her lovely blonde hair falling over her face. She pushed her hair back over her shoulders with an ease that just seems to come natural to women. She turned her head towards me and said, "Hi, Oliver." My heart racing, I'm sure I could hear those damned angels singing again. I said, "Hi Beth." She said, "Did I see Rueben just run by? He didn't say hello to me." She seemed really disappointed in the fact that Mill had not spoken to her.

Some bad thoughts started to cloud my mind. Did she like Milly more than me? She seemed quite upset that he hadn't spoken to her. I said, "I think he had to go somewhere with his mom." I thought Mill is going to kill me when he finds out that I have told Beth he had to go somewhere with his mommy. Anyway, Beth, talking about Milly..." She said, "Who's Milly?" I thought, oh, that's something else he will be mad about. I said, "Oh, that's Rueben's nickname." I could see him skulking at the top of the street, the swine. Before she could ask me why we called him Milly, I said, "Beth, he has asked me to give you this letter." She said, "Oh, this is a surprise." She held up the envelope to see what was written on the front, and there it was, 'Beth', written in bold italics.

The creep, I knew he was up to something. Let me guess, is he going to ask her for a date? I just know he is and I have just handed Beth with something that could destroy my chances with her. Milly might be a nice guy, and at certain angles he might be what you could call pretty. Pretty ugly, that is. Come on, Oliver. She's not going to choose a short guy with glasses, is she? She was still studying her name on the front of the envelope. She said, "Beautiful, isn't it?" I said, "Yes, I suppose it is." I had to agree with her. Milly must have put a lot of time and effort into just writing her name. God knows what he has put in the actual letter. The letters are about an inch high and they had coloured certain areas of each letter with blues and reds.

My curiosity got the better of me. I said, "Beth, are you going to open it?" She replied, "Yes, I think I will." She carefully opened the envelope. She said, "I don't want to damage it if I can help it." She lifted the flap of the envelope. And drew the letter out. She unfolded the letter and started to read. I watched as those beautiful green eyes darted from side to side as she scanned the letter. She stopped reading. I held my breath, she looked up at me and just went, "Oh, bless him, he has asked me for a date."

Before either of us could say anything, else I could hear what I could only describe as a sort of scrabbling, scratching sound. Beth's front door was about a quarter open and through that small gap something light brown with big eyes came flying through across the doorstep and onto the brick pathway, its claws trying to get a grip and failing on the smooth brickwork. Whatever it was bumped into the gate, finally seemed to get a grip, then disappeared back through the doorway. I said, "Beth, you have a rat problem. It came out of your front door and ran back in again." Beth said, "What did you say?" I very sheepishly replied, "Rat." With hands on hips, with a look that seemed to be between amusement and anger, if that's possible, she said, "How dare you call my chippy a rat!"

I then heard Beth's mom shout from inside their house,"Look out, Beth, he is having his mad half hour. I looked at Beth and smiled. I said,"Is she talking about you?" She started laughing and said no you fool, my dog. Mom's talking about my dog. I could hear that scrabbling noise then the rat came flying through the gap in the door again. It shot down the pathway. I could hear its tiny claws still trying to get a grip on the pathway. "Ah, here he is." She scooped up the little rat. I mean dog. Never having had a dog myself. I probably can't appreciate how much these pets mean to their owners. Obviously she adores her little dog, so I had better stop calling it a rat.

She held the little dog up in front of me. "How can you call him names? He is very sensitive. I hope he did not hear you call him a rat." The little dog looked up at me and started to growl showing those needle-like teeth. Dogs can't understand what we say and spell as well. Ridiculous, I have to admit, the little dog is very cute. Those big, round, almost black eyes, that little snout and bulbous forehead. What's not to like? I thought, right, this is where I could score Oliver points. So I attempted to stroke my new little doggy friend. Not a good idea, he nearly took my hand off. I remember reading about how the Aztecs or Incas used to adore these little pet dogs.

I thought, right, Oliver, you could save the day here. I said to Beth, "He is a chihuahua, isn't he?" I read something about these little dogs? The Aztecs? Or Incas. I could not remember which, they held them in very high esteem, so much so that when the owner died, they had their pet dogs buried with them. Because they could not bear being parted from them.

The not so nice part is generally the dogs were still alive when they buried them. Beth said, "Oh my god, how could they do that?" I replied, "I don't know, Beth." Beth smiled and said, "Oliver, I have to go now. See you tomorrow." I said, "Beth, is there anything I need to tell Milly?" "Oh yes, tell him I will have that date with him. I will see him on Saturday here outside my house." I said, "Ok, bye."

With that, I walked away as quickly as I could. I could not let Beth see the disappointment in my face and the tears in my eyes. I am certainly not letting Milly see me like this? I quickly brushed the tears away from my eyes with the back of my hand. Hopefully he won't see the pain he is causing me. I thought, come on, Oliver, pull yourself together. So I put a smile on my face and walked up to the corner where Milly was hiding.

I turned the corner. Milly's face lit up when he saw me. He started jumping up and down and shouting, "Well done Oliver." Well," Milly asked, "for Christ's sake Milly, stop jumping up and down. I delivered the words that almost stuck in my throat. Yes, Milly, she will see you outside her house tomorrow. With a big grin on his face, he started punching the air and twirling around shouting," Yes, yes, yes." After tomorrow he is going to be unbearable. I said, "Mill, I have got to go." Mill eventually calmed down and became quite serious. He looked into my face and said, "Oliver, are you ok?" Before I could answer, he gently punched me on my shoulder, and smiling said, "Best man won Oliver." I replied, "Of course, Mill, of course." Silly Milly then said, "Oliver, would you like to come with us?" I said, "No, I am not playing gooseberry. Anyway, it is Saturday tomorrow, I have a job to do for mom." "Ok, Oliver, see you on Sunday and thanks for what you did." And off he went. At first, I thought he was running but no, he was skipping and who can blame him?

I then went back home. I could not bring myself to go into the empty house, so I sat on the doorstep and waited for mom to come home. When she opened the front gate and saw me sitting on the step, she said, "Ok, what's the matter?" I replied, "Nothing, nothing." "Well come on in Oliver, and we will get some tea." "I'm not hungry, mom," I replied. "Oliver, come and sit down and talk to me." I said, "Mom, I just don't feel very well. I think I may be coming down with something." Mom just laughed and patted me on my knee and said, "Oliver, my very precious boy, haven't you ever noticed? You have never been ill in your life, not even the faintest sniffle." I had not thought about that before, but mom was right. She said, "You take after your father for that. He was incredibly hardy and as far as I know has never been ill." I said, "Mom, do you really, truly think dad will ever come back?" "Yes, Oliver, there is no doubt in my mind at all, he will come back to us. I don't know when exactly, but your father is a very honest and true man."

Mom explained to me that he would be away for a very long time and he really regretted having to leave us. "He told me what he had to do was very important and that he had no choice in the matter. I miss him terribly but knowing he will return gives me the strength to carry on. Oliver, your father absolutely adores you, have no doubt about that. You were three years old when he left. It absolutely broke his heart when he had to go. On the day he was leaving, he held you in his arms and with tears in his eyes he said, 'My beautiful son Oliver, please forgive me. I promise I will return as soon as I can.'" "But mom, I do not know what my own father looks like. There are no photographs of him or any of his family." "Oliver, I am sorry. I've told you this before, I do not have photos of your father and his family. There are photos of when you were a baby. Your father made me give a solemn promise that I would not have any photographs of him or his family around the house. Your father said to keep his identity a secret because there are certain people, if they knew what he looked like and learned of his identity could put us all in grave danger. There are also very important papers He needed to be kept safe. So your father gave me a special box to keep it all in, he said the box is indestructible and only he can open it." I jumped up and said, "I knew it. I just knew it, he's a spy, isn't he mom? Like James Bond? He is, isn't he, mom?" "Oliver, I honestly do not know, but I believe this is why he does not have contact with us for now. For fear of putting us all in danger."

I said to mom you know I feel much better about my dad now you have told me these things. You have even got me thinking that maybe he will come back one day." Mom said, "That's good, Oliver now tell me what is troubling you? You know you can tell me anything. After all, that's what moms are for." I said, "Mom, it's a bit awkward to talk to you about it." Mom just gave me a wry smile and said, "Is it that pretty girl who has just moved in at 27?" I looked at mom and smiled.

I said, "Ok mom, you got me." Mom said, "I spoke to her on my way home from work. She seems really nice and her name is Beth, isn't it?" I said, "Yes mom, her name is Beth Granger. Me and Mill met her. The problem is, mom, we both really like her." "well why don't you ask her out on a date?" "Too late, mom." With some bitterness in my voice, I said, "Mill has already got a date with her." "Well, bide your time. You know the saying. Faint heart never won a fair lady. You ask her out on a date. Then she can choose between you." I said, "Mom what if she doesn't want to date me?" Mom replied, "Oh, believe me, Oliver, she will go on a date with you." I said, "How are you so sure, mom?" She just tapped the side of her nose with her finger and said, "I know, I just know."

I looked at her, I said, "mom you haven't been to see Mrs Devere again?" "Yes, Oliver, she is a psychic medium and she is highly respected and very good at what she does. And before you scoff, Oliver, everything she has told me has been 100% accurate. "Mom she is supposedly talking to the dead." "Oliver, she does." "Mom, that's crazy when you're gone, you're gone". "Well, Oliver, I believe that a soul or spirit, whatever the case may be, does not die, when a body dies It transcends into the spiritual realms. Perhaps for infinity?" "Well, that's just gobbledygook to me, mom." "It may be gobbledygook to you but this may interest you. The very first time I went to see Mrs Devere, and remember, she was new to the area, she did not know me, or anything about me, I found her place in the town."

"It was Mrs Coyne, my boss from the cafe, who told me about her. She said she was absolutely brilliant. She said she told her things she could not have possibly known about. Well, that got my curiosity. So when I walked into her place I was a bit nervous. When I opened the door, on my left were shelves full of different types of crystals, there were paintings of various sizes, mostly of North American Indians, and beautiful paintings of wolves. There were things hanging from the ceiling that looked to me like tennis rackets without the handles. There were lots of feathers hanging off them. I later found they were called dream catchers. There was a small counter to the right as you walked in. On the wall at the back of the counter were more shelves full of figurines mostly of North American Indians. On the counter was a beautiful bust of an Indian, life-size, carved out of wood."

I said, "Mom, what's a bust?" "Head and shoulders to you. I thought that would get your interest, Oliver. Ok, can you get to the point, mom?" "Patience now, if you will let me carry on. After I had finished looking around, I noticed a doorway in front of me with those beady things hanging in the doorway, you know, those things that rattle when you walk through them. It was very quiet and I was feeling very nervous. So I shouted, 'Hello. Anybody there ?' Then I heard a voice from the other side of the curtain. 'Is that Alice, come through?' So I walked through the beaded curtain into the room and I was pleasantly surprised because in my mind I had expected to see a typical gypsy Rose Lee type character, but she was completely the opposite.

I was greeted by this warm, friendly person who made me feel relaxed straight away. The only typical gypsy thing I could see was this small round table that she was sitting at with a crystal ball in the centre. The room was really nice. Besides the table there was a carved table with ornaments on it, and a leather settee against the far wall. She asked me to sit down and immediately started to give me a reading. She gave me information which was surprisingly accurate. She told me I had had a very private wedding, which was true. She told me my husband had been away from home for a long time and would be returning. But could not say when, this I completely understood. Then she said, 'You have one child, a boy, a very special boy. He is different from all other children. When he is about 16, for some reason, I see him doing lots of travelling and I mean lots of travelling. I feel he will have a companion, someone quite extraordinary. Why do I keep hearing something like olives? Does he like to eat them? Horrible things.' I had to laugh and I said no , no, my son's name is Oliver, then she said, 'I also have the name Milly. Would this be a girl your son knows?' "

I said to mom, "Did she really think Milly was a girl?" "Yes, Oliver, she did, but I corrected her and told her that he was a boy and his nickname is Milly, but his real name is Rueben. And he is your best friend." I said, "No, mom. He is a big girl's blouse and he is not my friend." "Now, now, Oliver. You know you could not have a better friend. Don't you think that is very unkind, calling him a big girl's blouse whatever that means." Then I saw mom put her hand over her mouth and I knew the way her head and shoulders were shaking. She was laughing, and she was trying to stifle the laughter by putting her hand over her mouth, then she let out this howl of laughter which I had never heard from my mother before. It was infectious.

The next I knew we were both rolling around laughing our heads off. With tears in her eyes, mom said, "Come on Oliver, let's stop laughing now. " Wiping the tears from her eyes, she said, Ok I will finish the message. Mrs Devere gave me because this part is for you, Oliver. She told me that you would meet a very pretty young girl and you would both fall in love at first sight. She said she felt a strong spiritual link with this girl but could not understand why. Oliver I believe that girl is Beth. Although I think you are too young, it seems my little boy's falling in love."

Milly and Beth had gone to a Saturday afternoon matinee. I didn't know what films they had gone to see and if I am honest, I don't care. But I did stand in front of the window overlooking the street with my nose up against mom's best net curtains. I knew roughly what time the matinee finished and it would take about 20 minutes to walk back from the cinema to Beth's.

I had calculated they should pass my house not long after 4:00. well, it's twenty minutes past four, still no sign, where the hell are they? After another five minutes they suddenly appeared. I could see their heads bobbing up and down over the top of our privet hedge, I could hear them chatting away. I mean, what could they talk about? They have not got anything in common, unless Beth is interested in Milly's toy soldiers, and marble collection, ha. I don't think so. They were now slowly passing our front gate. They both stopped and turned and looked up at the window I was standing at. Milly the swine waved. Beth just smiled.

I quickly ducked down below the window sill. Oh god, I hope they didn't see me. They must both be thinking how pathetic I am. Well, I will find out tomorrow. I said I would meet Milly in the park on Sunday morning. I could not wait .Next day I saw him on one of the kiddies' swings. When he saw me a big grin appeared on his face. How smug can you get? I walked up behind him and grabbed the swing to stop him moving. In his right ear, I said, come on, Mill, spill the beans, Mill told me they had a great day. He had paid for them to go in. I said, "Let me guess, Beth paid for the popcorn and drinks." Mill replied, Yes, but she insisted." Laughing, I said you skinflint." Mill said, "Ok, Ok, but it is a good job that she did as I had no more money." I said, "Ok Mill, I believe you."

I gripped him by the shoulders, shook him a couple of times, and looking through those big thick glasses of his, into those very dark, shiny eyes, I said, "What did you talk about? But more importantly, did you kiss Beth?" He shook himself free of my grip. Then he snapped back at me. "Do you really want to know what Beth talked about all the way to the cinema? Most of the film and all the way back was Oliver this, Oliver that," shaking his head from side to side and pulling a face. "Oliver, she just gave me a blinking headache."

I said, "But did you kiss her?" Hands on his hips, still shaking his head from side to side, quite comical, our Milly is. He replied, "Oliver, you will be happy to know, I tried to, but she just said 'no, no, no, Rueben behave.' Then grabbed me by my ears, pulled my head forward and kissed my forehead.

She thanked me for taking her out. I thought, shall I ask her for another date? Then I thought better of it." Then Mill said sarcastically, "Oliver, are you happy now?"

I just stood there, stunned by what Milly had just told me. Then I had this warm, wonderful feeling come over me. I said, "Mill, do you really think Beth likes me?" "Jesus, Oliver, do you need it in writing? She's crazy about you." "I am sorry, Mill but I really do think I may be in love with her. Boy, that sounds sloppy." "Oliver, I know you do. I could tell by the way you were looking at her something serious was going on. She was so gorgeous I had to try, but deep down I know she was not really interested in me."

I said, "Mill, I got really mad when I knew you were going on a date with Beth. I thought I had lost my chance with her. You know, mom said I would not get a better friend than you, Mill. She was 100% right. If there weren't so many people about Mill, I would give you a big sloppy kiss." Mill's response was 'Aarrgh' then I was brought to a sudden stop because I thought I could hear angels singing like mom said I would hear if I happened to fall in love with somebody. but no.no angels, just an ice cream van, I stood there and clenched my fists and went 'yes, yes'. People started looking at me so I had better go. I shouted, "Wait for me, Mill." My heart was pounding as I tried to catch up with Mill. He will either get a big sloppy kiss or I will strangle him. Not necessarily in that order. Whichever makes him suffer the most.

As I was leaving through the park gates there was a sweet shop on the opposite corner and who do you think was coming out of the sweet shop? Milly, Milly no Money, he was sucking on an ice lolly, and another one in his left hand. After accepting the bribe, we walked down the road sucking on our lollies. Milly getting a brain freeze serves him right. When we were about halfway down our lollies, we decided to lean against the wall of Mr Gilbert's house. It had been another hot, sunny day. And the wall felt really warm on our backs and shoulders. I tilted my head back and closed my eyes, the sunlight penetrating my eyelids, making me see this lovely orange colour.

I heard Mill's voice sounding as if he was half asleep. Very dreamily, he said, "This Mr Gilbert will be angry if he finds us leaning on his wall." I replied, Mill, let's put it this way. If he wants to catch us, he will never do it in a million years." Mill said very slowly, "Why Olly?" Which instantly made me think of Laurel and Hardy. I replied, "Another fine mess you've got me into, Stanley." That made both of us burst out laughing. Milly said, "What makes you think Mr Gilbert couldn't catch us, Olly?" While he was saying this he did the famous hair pinching gesture made by Stanley.

Now, for some reason we had suddenly turned into Laurel and Hardy. So I replied, "Well, Stanley, Mr Gilbert is not a very tall person. He is also a very round person, just like looking at a football with a tennis ball on top. He looks just like a very big owl. He has a sharp nose which looks like an owl's beak and he wears those big round glasses, making him look as if he has these huge eyes." Still laughing when we heard what sounded like a front door slamming, I said, "Run Stanley, I think the owl is after us." Milly replied "I'm right behind you, Olly." While running, Milly looked behind him and said, "You were right Olly, he does look like an owl."

We reached the top of my street totally out of breath but still laughing. Milly said, "See you tomorrow Olly." As he runs towards home? I shouted after him. "Stop calling me Olly, Stanley." He just laughed and carried on. I stood at the top of the street looking and listening for the sound of that squeaky gate, a sound I have learned to love. There was nothing. So

I made my way home. I had just got to my front gate when I heard that familiar squeak banging sound of her gate.

Did I imagine it? No. There it was again. My heart leapt. I felt myself smiling. I had to go to her and tell her how I feel before I chicken out. I started to walk down to her house but before I had got there Beth's beautiful head popped out over the gate brushing her long blonde hair back off her face. She looked up at me and with a smile said "Hi Oliver, are you coming to see me?" As I approached her squeaky garden gate, she stepped back a few feet and I noticed she had this devilish twinkle in her eyes. I was greeted by this wonderful smile. I had the feeling that Beth could be very mischievous. I replied the answer to your question is, yes, I have come to see you Beth with her hands clasped in front of her, she said very softly "is there something you want to ask me, Oliver?"

My heart was pounding and my hands were shaking. Then she made things worse by throwing her head back, and pushing her hair back over her shoulders then shaking her head from side to side. Mesmerised, I was completely dumb struck. She put her hand over her mouth and started chuckling. I realised she was just teasing me. So I thought, right, Beth Granger? I plucked up my courage, reached over the gate, grabbed her hand, which took her by surprise. I said, "I have now had the courage to hold your hand and I'm going to ask you, Beth, do you like me?"

She seemed to hesitate, then said something completely unexpected. She replied, "Oliver no, I do not like you." My face must have been a picture. Then, grinning, Beth said, "No, Oliver, I love you." "What?? What did you say?" "I said I love you, Oliver. By the way Oliver, you're hurting my hand." "Oh my god, Beth, I am so sorry." I released her hand but she would not let go. Beth said, "I know it is difficult for you, males, to say the 'love' word. But I know you love me, Oliver. It was love at first sight and I believe it was the same for you."

Still holding her hand, I looked into her beautiful face and just got lost in those big beautiful green eyes. Very emotionally I said, "I do love you, Beth." I thought, my god, have I just said that? "The second I saw you, I knew and you just took my breath away." Beth said, laughing, "I sort of noticed that, but you are all right now." "No, Beth, my nerves are shot to pieces." We both laughed at that. I was still holding her hand when Beth said to me "Oliver, you are trembling". You do not ever have to be afraid of me." I said, that is alright for you to say. The only other person in the world that I have said 'I love you to' is my mom and then to say 'I love you' to the most beautiful girl I've ever seen in my life. I would be crazy not to be nervous.

Beth said, "I find you very beautiful as well." I felt the colour come up into my face. My face must have been crimson. Beth said" Oh god, Oliver, I've embarrassed you. I am really sorry, but you were so shy and nervous and I so wanted you to ask me out. It was the only thing I could think of to spur you into action and I think it may have worked out, wouldn't you agree, Oliver. As my colour started to get back to normal, there was a question I had to ask Beth. I said, "If you feel that way about me, why did you have a date with Milly?" "Because the first time I met you, I know how you felt about me."

Beth suddenly became quite serious. And said to me, "Do you believe in karma? Do you believe that our lives are already mapped out for us? What will be?" will be! She took me by surprise again. I said, "Beth, I don't really know." Then, Beth said, "Please don't laugh at me, but I already knew I was going to meet you, that we would fall in love at first sight. I have had visions of you, Oliver, long before I came to live here. So you see, Oliver, I knew I was meant to be here, at this place at this time, you were always my true destiny, my true love." She continued, "Did you know the old lady that used to live in the house?" I replied, "Beth, me and mom, didn't have much to do with her. She was rather the sort of person that appeared to like her own company. She would go out once a week to do her shopping, and that's really the only time we saw her. Mom being mom felt sorry for her and one day knocked on her door. Mom offered to do shopping for her but before mom could say anything else, Mrs Morgan snapped at mom 'I don't need any help, thank you very much.' And slammed the door in mom's face. But in her defence, she had lost her husband in the First World War and her only son in the Second World War." Beth said, "How terrible for her. So you would not say she could have been in any way at all a kind or generous person." I replied, "No way? I do not know of any person that she gave anything to or was kind to."

Beth said, "Well, what I'm about to tell you may surprise and amaze you. Mrs Morgan left the house and contents to my father in her will." I said, "Oh, she is a relative of yours then." "No, Oliver that is what is so strange, she is not a relative and no member of our family has ever met her or any of her family. Dad was very grateful to Mrs Morgan. But equally just as baffled as to why a perfect stranger would leave her whole house to him. So dad asked a friend who is into all this genealogy stuff to see if there's any link between the two families. Dad's friend got back to him. He said he had managed to trace both families' histories quite a way back and as far as he could tell there is no connection." "I don't know what shocked me the most - you having visions of me or Mrs Morgan being so generous." "Now, Oliver, you are just mocking me." "No Beth, if I am honest there has been a lot of strange things happening around me and Milly. One time three boys were chasing me and Mill. They were grabbed by their ankle and thrown quite a distance of about thirty or forty feet into a stream. Really weird. Milly had a fright in the alleyway where he saw a face in the wall, and it jumped out at him. I had been having weird, frightening nightmares. No wonder they call the town Wytchwood. So you had a vision about me?"

Beth replied, "Yes, in my vision, I heard the name of Oliver and I saw you as clear as I am seeing you now. You think I am crazy, don't you, Oliver?" I replied, "No, never. It's just that you sound very much like this crazy, weird woman mom goes to see in the town. She's a psychic or a medium, something like that - a Mrs Devere." I had been holding Beth's hand all the time. We had been talking but she suddenly let go of my hand. Hands on hips and with a withering look, she said, "Do you mind?" I thought to myself, oh no, another fine mess you've got yourself into, Olly. She said, "It's ok, Oliver. Even I think I am weird and crazy as well."

I thought, phew, how did I get away with that one? I think I may have a mischievous pixie on my hands here. Beth said Mom believes I have the gift as well. I put my hand to my forehead, and said, oh no I have done it again. "I am really sorry, Beth." She turned her back on me, and said, "So you should be sorry." She turned back to me, laughing. Still smiling, she said to me, "Do you believe in guardian angels, Oliver?"

I thought to myself, careful, Oliver, this could be a trick question. Remember no foot in the mouth answers. So I replied quite cleverly, or so I thought, back at you Beth, "Do you believe in guardian angels?" Beth just looked at me and with a puzzled look on her face, replied, "Oliver, I am asking you, and by the way, yes, I do believe that everybody has a guardian angel." I said, "Ok Beth. Honest answer, no, I don't believe in them."

Little did I realise that in the near future my answer to that question will come to bite me in the bum, as the saying goes. I said, "Beth, if I had a guardian angel don't you think my angel would have stopped all the bullying that me, Mill and other kids have to go through every day. Stopped Jake the snake from punching me in the nose? And knocking me out. And stopped all the bullying. I mean, we get punched and kicked, called names, money stolen off us. The bigger kids even steal our lunch."

I threw my hands up towards the sky and said, "come on, angels, where are you"? Beth laughed and said, perhaps it is because you do not believe in them that they don't visit you." I said, yes, Beth. Maybe you are right. Milly says your mom is nice. Yes, Salt of the earth, since we have been here, mom has managed to get a job as a secretary. I asked "How about your dad, Beth? Has he got a job here?" Beth just shook her head and became quite serious. She said dad can't work, he is quite ill" Sorry, Beth, can't the doctors do anything for him?

⊷≼◆≽⊶

Butter Melting Kiss

Beth replied he has been to see so many doctors and specialists, but none of them seemed to know what is wrong with my dad. Dad had his own business making small components for the sports car industry. He just suddenly became ill. He found he could not walk, he was having problems with his hands and arms, and dad lost his business. We could not pay the mortgage and lost our house as well. When everything seemed to be falling about our ears, Dad got this solicitor's letter informing him that this house had been left to him in a lady's will. What a shock! But that had come just at the right time. The strange thing is dad's health seems to be improving since we moved here." I said to Beth, "I've got to ask you this. Was there any particular car that your dad made parts for?"

Beth cupped her hand and whispered in my ear, "Let's put it this way, Oliver, James Bond appears to be quite fond of this car." "Wow, I was trying to work out which had the most effect on me. Her warm breath on my cheek and ear, or her closeness to me, or her dad making parts for the James Bond car." I think Beth may have won hands down.

When she came close to me, she had this wonderful sweet scent about her, and I was very tempted to kiss her. Then I thought better of it. She would probably tell me to behave, grab me by my ears and kiss me on the forehead like she did with Milly. But I could hear mom's words in my head. Remember, a faint heart never won a fair lady. Beth just said,

"Oliver, I have to go now." She was making her way towards her front door. I waited till Beth was clear of her garden gate and with mom's words ringing in my ears, I quickly opened the gate.

The squeaky gate gave me away and Beth turned around very quickly and said, "Oliver, what are you doing?" I said, "Nothing," and with my heart beating like crazy I slid my hands around her beautifully slim waist and pulled her tightly against me. I could feel the warmth of her body. She did not say anything, she just looked into my eyes. Then I kissed her. Those incredibly warm soft lips just sent me into seventh heaven. I just wanted this moment never to end. I just could not bring myself to let her go. I suddenly felt Beth appear to go slightly limp and for a few seconds she just seemed to hang in my arms, but I need not have worried because she seemed to recover and kissed me back with so much passion, it made me go dizzy. Then I felt Beth pull back slightly separating our lips from that wonderful first passionate kiss.

Smiling, she looked up at me and very quietly whispered, "Oliver I have to go." Reluctantly, I released her out of my arms. She then grabbed both of my hands, pulled me towards her and gave me a quick kiss on the lips. Laughing, she said, "I am going. She quickly ran to her front door. Before she opened the door, she turned back towards me. She didn't say anything but I noticed she had tears in her eyes. Before I could say anything, she mouthed the words. Love you, Oliver"

I quickly looked around to make sure that nobody was watching. Then I thought, who cares if anybody is watching, so I mouthed the words, "Love you Beth see you tomorrow." Beth opened the door and went inside. I started to make my way back home. It is a good job, I only live a few doors away, as I was feeling very weak at the knees. As I reached my garden gate, I thought to myself, Oliver, what is happening to you? You are a man, well, a boy man, anyway. You have gone all sloppy, like a big girl's blouse. I can never understand why they say that. Still, it seems like I have become one.

I leaned forward with my arms resting on top of the gate. I tried to work out just what had happened to me. You have just fallen in love with the most beautiful girl in the world. Dork, that's what has happened to you and apparently she loves you. Well, I have this wonderful feeling inside. I feel the happiest I've ever been in my life. After serious consideration, I am now the biggest girl's blouse in the world, and I do not care. I opened the gate and went in for my tea.

It's Monday, school day again. Some of the lessons I look forward to. Now when I wake up in the morning, I cannot wait to go to school. Do you want to know why? Well, I walk with Beth to school in the morning. Then I walk back home with her, fantastic. Milly continued to walk with me and Beth to school but after a few days realised he was playing gooseberry. So he decided he would go to school on his own, taking the shorter route that we used to take before. I tried to tell him myself and Beth did not mind him walking to school with us, but he was being stubborn, as usual, and once he had made his mind up, I'm afraid that was it, I said, "Ok, Mill, just be careful." You see, the street Milly has to walk down is a street the Garnetts live on and I worry about Jake the snake catching hold of Milly. The Garnetts' house is towards the top of the street and their garden backs on to the alleyway. There is no way Mill will go down the alley again after the experience he had, but Mill told me he runs as fast as he can up the street and always on the opposite side to the Garnetts.

I said to Beth, "It really is sad when our life is ruled and ruined by bullies. Perhaps one day they will get their comeuppance." Beth replied, "There is no doubt in my mind that they will, some sooner than others." It was strange the way she said that. Oh well, it is not for me to reason why. Perhaps she knows something I don't. Needless to say, our relationship blossomed, and I saw Beth as often as I could. Beth's mom and dad had no problem at all with me seeing her. I explained to mom how I felt about Beth, and if she was ok with it?

Mom looked at me with her usual knowing smile and said, "Oliver, you are my son, my only child. It is obvious I want and need you to be happy, content and safe in life. Beth appears to be the person that can give you all that, Beth is a lovely, sweet girl. I could not be happier for you." Well, with the green light from our parents we took full advantage. We were surrounded by beautiful countryside and would go for walks down country lanes. We would hold hands and just talk about anything and everything, and occasionally we would kiss. In my opinion, too much walking and not enough kissing. I think Beth was rationing me. Perhaps that's the way she was thinking. We would also go for walks on our local common. It was a beautiful place.

There were tarmac pathways that wound their way around and through the common, one of the pathways led to this lovely little chapel set in this hollow of the common. On the one side of the chapel there was a gentle slope with clumps of pine trees dotted here and there. There was a small clearing between the trees and we would often go for picnics there. We would take a flask, some sandwiches and some of mom's cakes.

It was on one of these picnics I asked Beth, did she realise that she had gone limp in my arms for a few seconds? And she really worried me. She just looked straight ahead, and seemed to be thinking. Was she recollecting that moment? She then turned to me and with a dreamy look on her face said, "My dear wonderful Oliver, the reason I went limp in your arms is because your warm, tender kiss just made me [melt like butter.] I thought she was just winding me up. I said, "Honest Beth?" "Yes, Oliver, that is the effect you had on me." My ego just took a huge leap. I wonder if I could tell Milly about my super hot butter melting kisses. Better not, I think Beth would kill me.

I was just about to give Beth another [butter melting kiss] when I heard a familiar voice. The voice said, now, now, behave yourself. You have company. It was Milly, He was standing about 10 feet away partly obscured by the pine trees. What wasn't obscured though, was this smug wide grin on his face. I thought, what is he up to now? I did not have to wait long. Purring like a cat Milly said, "Hello, Beth. Hello, Oliver. I want you to meet someone." I realised he was holding someone's hand, but we had not seen her as she was behind a tree. "Yes, I did say a she." Milly and this very pretty dark-haired girl walked towards us. Well, I was lost for words. Beth said, "Come and sit down. We have got sandwiches and some cakes, if you would like some." I moved over to let Milly sit by my side,and the girl sat down beside Milly. Beth said, "Well, Rueben introduce us then." Milly replied, "Oh, sorry this is Ruby, my girlfriend." As he was saying the word 'girlfriend', his head slowly rotated towards me.

Milly grinning from ear to ear, and over the top of his glasses I could see those two big black caterpillars he calls eyebrows, doing the rumba. He did not need to say anything. Those dancing eyebrows and grin told me everything, which is, "Look at me, Oliver, bet ya did not expect that." Little did he realise that I'm really glad that he has finally got a girlfriend. I was getting a bit worried about him as except for school, I rarely saw him at other times. Well, there was no need for me to be concerned because after introductions to each other, he then drops another bombshell.

It appears our Milly has been going to karate lessons, and this is where he met Ruby. "Wow," is all I can say. Apparently they had been seeing each other for about a month. The way they looked at each other and with Milly's arm wrapped around her, I had the feeling it was quite serious. Beth and Ruby were getting along like a house on fire, perhaps buckets of water, brain to Oliver, behave yourself. Mill seemed to be doing well at karate. His instructor told him he has potential. Well, there are a few ladybirds and caterpillars in our garden he could do his karate chops on. Better not though, he could get hurt. I should not mock him just in case he can really do karate. Milly is still with Ruby, which is great.

We go out quite a lot as a foursome, still getting bullied at school though..one good thing, me and Mill leave school this year. Done with our exams. Milly is top of his class in virtually everything. Me top of my class in science, maths and generally good most other subjects. Clever clogs Milly I believe maybe going to college. Me, I'm not sure. Perhaps find my dad and save the world. How ironic if my dad is a secret agent. I could join him fighting the bad guys in the world. That's, of course, if mom would let me. Beth said she would like to go to college to study archaeology. Beautiful and brainy, my Beth. Milly's girlfriend Ruby has decided she would like to be a nurse.

Mom told me not to worry about my future or career at the moment as she believes that something will present itself to me. That will be very interesting and exciting and may include travelling. It will also be very rewarding. "Mom," I said, "stop rolling your eyes and tutting. You have been to see that spooky medium woman again, haven't you?" Mom replied, "Yes, I needed to know things and she is very good." "Oh mom, so that's where all that's come from. All this so-called interesting, exciting travelling job. I am going to be a salesman now. Thank you." "Now don't be silly Oliver. I know you are meant to be doing something very special and important with your life. I am sure you believe that as well, Oliver."

Mom was right, as usual. I smiled and said, "Ok mom, but I still don't believe somebody can talk to the dead. That's just crazy." "Ok, Oliver, if that is what you think. That's not a problem but I know there will come a day when you will believe. As it happens, Oliver, you will be meeting Mrs Devere yourself tomorrow. You see I owe Mrs Devere some money from my last reading. You know I do not like owing money to anyone if I can help it. Mrs Devere very kindly told me not to worry about the money as it was a free one. On the house, as they say. But you know me and my principles. So will you please take the money down to her tomorrow, Oliver?" "Ok, mom. I will go down first thing in the morning." Oliver, she is very much like Beth so you will feel right at home." "Yes, mom." Ok, I thought to myself, I am not looking forward to that at all.

Well it's Saturday morning "I'm just going to get ready now mom, as Beth, Milly, Ruby and I are going to the pictures. Be back at about twelve, ok, mom." I heard mom's voice from the kitchen. "Ok, Oliver, just tell me when you are going." With that, I got myself all spruced up and ready to go. As I was going through the front door, I shouted to mom, "Going now." Mom replied, "Have a nice time and watch what you are doing."

I made my way down to Beth's. She was just coming out of her front door. She looked stunning. I said "Hi Beth." She replied, "Hello, Oliver." I said, "Wow!" "And wow to you Oliver." We stood talking for a while and after about 10 minutes, Milly and Ruby joined us. Ruby looked really pretty. She wore this long dress, as Beth wore a short skirt and a pretty frilly white blouse.

Milly looked very smart with his dark blue shirt and black trousers compared to my light blue shirt and black trousers. He always tries to copy what I wear. I don't mind. They say imitation is the sincerest form of flattery. If you squint your eyes in the dark, Milly looked almost handsome. I was surprised because he did look really good. He looked so shiny as if somebody had buffed him up. His hair was all slicked back and his nose was so shiny, I could see my face in it.

Milly and I take the mickey out of each other, but we have a very special friendship, and nothing or nobody will ever break that bond between us. Unless he tries to run off with my woman, that's different. Anyway, we started to make our way to the picture house. We're about halfway down our street when Milly suddenly stopped and said, "Listen." So we all stopped and listened. Nothing, except for a few birds singing and traffic noise in the distance. I said, "Mill, what are we listening for?" Milly replied, "I could hear a noise when we were walking, but it has stopped now. It sounded like a [clicking] or [clunking] noise, a bit like the noise of blind man's cane makes when he taps the walls or floor." I said, Mill, Beth and Ruby are wearing high heels. Could that be the noise?" "No, no, Oliver, this was definitely behind us"Ok Mill we will have to get moving or we will miss the beginning of the film. So we started to walk at a fast pace.

We reached the main road and we hadn't gone very far and while we were still walking, Beth suddenly said, "Oliver I can hear a clicking noise behind us." We stopped and turned around very quickly, hoping to see whoever or whatever might be following us. Or god forbid, stalking us. Because just lately strange things have been going on. It has started to unnerve me a little. We stood still, watching and listening. There was no clicking noise, not a soul to be seen. An occasional car would pass by. But that was it, there was absolutely nothing, and I mean nothing. We had a clear view down this long straight road, there were houses on one side of the road and the majority had walls or fences to their front gardens. The speed with which we had turned around there is no way that somebody could have jumped over a wall, or fence to avoid being seen. It was impossible.

What is really weird and frightening is that the clicking sound carried on for a few seconds after we had turned. Then very abruptly stopped. I could see the girls were getting very frightened and they were not the only ones. I could feel the hairs on the back of my neck standing up. Ruby had been very quiet up till now, but with a shaky voice said, "I think we should phone the police." Mill said, "I agree with Ruby." Then Beth started laughing and said, "What do we tell the police? That we have a strange clicking sound following us. They will think we are crazy."

Mill piped up, "Whatever is making that clicking noise might be watching us right now, and if that clicking starts again, I do not want to be standing here." Mill cautiously looked around him then suddenly said, "I think we should run fast." Ruby said, "We can't run. We are wearing high heels." I said, "Beth, Ruby, take off your shoes. Like Milly said, we should run and get away from here." The girls took their shoes off. I think Ruby was too frightened to be embarrassed when she had to hitch her skirt up to her knees.

We just ran as fast as we could. After about ten minutes, Milly breathlessly said, "Stop, stop, I need to catch my breath." Then Milly, breathing heavily, said, "Listen. I can't hear it anymore. It's gone," and in the same breath, "oh Jesus, I can hear it in the distance, but this time, whatever it is appears to be running." The girls screamed and we all started running again. I shouted, "Keep going. The picture house is only a few hundred yards away. Turn right into that street up ahead." We eventually turned into the street, gasping for breath. The cinema is only about fifty yards away but that last fifty yards felt like forever.

As we approached the cinema entrance, I noticed Charlie, the doorman having a quiet cigarette. Me and Milly used to come to the Saturday matinees and got to know Charlie quite well. He was always polite but very strict if you misbehaved in the cinema. He wasn't a very tall man, he had dark hair and wore these heavy horn-rimmed glasses. Always smart with this light red jacket trimmed with gold. Always sharp creases in his black trousers, his black shoes highly polished. When we first saw him, we noticed he had quite a bad limp. I had asked the ticket lady why he had a limp. She replied quite cheerfully, "Oh, he has a club foot, dear. If you look at one of his shoes, it has been built up. I believe he was born like that." "How sad" I said. I still do not know what a clubfoot is, but I always felt sorry for Charlie because some of the kids who went to the Saturday matinee would mock him and call him names. Children can be very cruel at times. He had just finished his cigarette and was about to go back into the cinema. I shouted, "Charlie wait." He stopped and turned around. Recognising me, he smiled and said, "Hello Oliver." When he saw the others, still smiling, he said, "Hi there," but his smile faded when he saw how frightened we all were, especially the girls. "What the hell is the matter? You all look as if you have seen a ghost." "That's the problem, Charlie. Something or somebody appears to be stalking us. We can hear whatever it is, but we can't see anything. We can just hear this strange clicking or clunking sound, and it always seemed to keep a set distance away from us. We are really worried about going back home later." Charlie said listen, "I will go up to the main road and have a look to see if I can see anything. Go in and get your tickets. I'll be back in a minute."

I said to Mill, "Get my ticket for me. I'll go with Charlie. I can't let him go on his own." Mill replied, "Ok, Oliver." When I looked around Charlie was already up there, standing in the middle of the main road. Then I saw him quickly go to the far side of the road. Standing on the pavement there, looking in all directions. I shouted across to him, "Can you see anything, Charlie?" He just shrugged his shoulders, arms outstretched, hands, palms up, just said, "Nothing, absolutely nothing." He crossed back over the road towards me, "Sorry, Oliver. I could not see or hear anything, but there was a hell of a fishy smell over the road there." "Strange, mom says she gets a smelly fishy odour as well every so often. Thanks Charlie, I am very grateful." Charlie replied in his usual cheerful way, "No problem, Oliver, but I think you had better hurry and get into the cinema or you will miss the film."

We tried to enjoy the film as best as we could. I think for all of us what had happened earlier was still strong in our minds. I thanked Charlie again as we very hesitantly exited through the cinema doors. We had decided we would go a different way home. As most of the cinema goers were going that way we felt much safer. We tried to listen for that clicking sound but because of the chatter from the other people, we would not have heard it anyway. As we walked back we talked about the film we had just watched. It was Peter Pan, it was really enjoyable. We tried to sandwich ourselves between as many people as we could, but frighteningly the people we were with were mostly couples, they started to peel off in different directions, eventually leaving us on our own. We watched the last couple disappear.

We stood still, and listened and to our relief, silence except for an owl to wit, to woo in the tree above our heads, making us nearly jump out of our skins. We made our way back home. Ruby first. We made sure she was safely in her house. See you tomorrow Ruby." We continued on to Milly's. Milly said, "See you tomorrow, Beth, Oliver." We replied, "See you tomorrow." He disappeared into his house. I then walked Beth back home, stopping every so often to listen. It seemed, whatever was following us had given up. "Thank god," I said to Beth, "don't you think it is strange that it was only us that the thing or person seemed to be stalking." We finally reached Beth's house.

She opened that squeaky gate of hers Beth closed it and faced me. I looked into those beautiful eyes and was lost once more. God, have I got it bad. It was only Beth's voice calling my name that brought me back. Beth said, "Oliver, I am talking to you. You were miles away." "Beth, I am sorry, but it is your fault." "My fault?" Beth said in a slightly raised voice and pointing to herself. I said to Beth, "You seem to have this hypnotic effect on me." She just bowed her head and started laughing, she lifted her head, still laughing. She said, "I hypnotise you, do I? When we are married, I should have no problem getting you to do all the household chores."

I replied, "Whatever happens, I will always be under your spell. I believe you are a beautiful witch in disguise." Beth said, "Oliver, how did you guess?" I know she was just mocking me. "Yes, Oliver, the answer to your question. I do find it strange that it seemed to be targeting just us and nobody else. None of the people at the cinema had mentioned anything unusual and we were walking and talking with crowds of people," Beth said with a worried look on her face. "You don't think it is just one of us it is after, do you?" I replied that had crossed my mind and in its own way, makes it a bit more frightening.

Beth then said, "As far as I am aware, I don't think I have any enemies. We couldn't have imagined it, could we? I mean, we didn't see anything or anybody, but I have to be honest, Oliver, I can't explain it. I did have the feeling that something was there. Nothing tangible, nothing I could put my finger on. I felt a presence there so when I said could we have imagined it, I am sure that I didn't.

I think I was just deluding myself, hoping I will be able to get some sleep tonight. I was really frightened Oliver, especially when Milly shouted it was running. It sounded like somebody on the typewriter typing very fast, repeatedly, on one key. I think Ruby was even more frightened than I was." She was holding my hand at the time and when she heard that noise, she nearly crushed my hand.

I said, "Beth, promise you won't freak out if I tell you something?" Beth replied, "I couldn't get much more freaked out than I am now. So you might as well tell me. I probably won't sleep much tonight anyway." I said, "Beth, are you sure?" "Oliver, please, I am sure." "You know Beth when we first started hearing that noise, well, I had the strangest feeling in my back and spine. My back had been hurting me in the night, and because of it I didn't get much sleep. So that strange feeling in my back, I just did not think a lot of it at the time. It was when we started to run that I had this strong tugging sensation in my back and spine. It really unnerved me because the faster I ran the stronger that tugging sensation seemed to become. Somehow I feel different. I don't feel like me anymore."

I think just to reassure me, Beth said, you still look and sound like my Oliver, the Oliver I am deeply in love with. So if you turn into a monster, I will still love you." She just laughed.

"Thank you, Beth. Ditto." She just gently punched me on my shoulder. I said, "Beth, before you go, I just wanted to tell you how grateful I am to the powers that be for bringing you into my life. I have to be the luckiest boy in the world. But I really do have to tell you this. It may be connected to what happened tonight.

Me and Mill have a common enemy and he just lives about three quarters of the way up the alleyway. We have had quite a few encounters with him. I know it was him that wrecked poor Mr. O' Conner's house. I had looked into his eyes not long before he had hit me and I could see just absolute pure evil and I know when he gets the opportunity he means to do me and Mill serious harm. I am convinced he is not of this world. I don't think he is even human. Whatever he is, he walks with the devil." "Well, Oliver, I have to thank you for that extra bit of information that I really could have done without, Beth said. "I now have something that follows me, that I can hear, but I cannot see, and now you tell me there's a maniac that lives not far from where I live. Well, sweet dreams to you, Oliver, because I certainly won't be having any sleep, will I?" With that she turned on her heel and started to walk up the pathway.

I said, "Beth, haven't you forgotten something?" She turned and said, "Oh, and what would that be, Oliver?" I pulled a face and pointed to my lips. "Oh, you want to be rewarded after half frightening me to death?" "Well, if you don't kiss me, I won't be able to sleep tonight either, Beth." Then she walked slowly towards me, flung her arms around my neck and very passionately kissed me, and this time it was [me that melted like butter]. Note to brain, frighten Beth more often.

It was a very long kiss, then Beth patted me on my shoulders. I think it was a signal for me to let go of her and once more, very reluctantly, I did just that. I said, "Beth, if that was punishing me I'm really looking forward to when you are going to be nice to me." Beth said, "In your dreams, Oliver, in your dreams." I just laughed. Then I asked Beth if she would like to come with me to her aunt, Mrs Devere, to her shop in the town tomorrow morning. I explained that mom owed Mrs Devere some money and had asked me to take it to her. I said, "Mom just does not like owing money to anybody." Beth said, "Sorry Oliver, I promised mom I would help her with her shopping tomorrow, but I will see you later, ok? About 2:00 tomorrow afternoon. I really have to go." She then ran up to her front door, turned and blew me a kiss, and was gone.

I walked back home still trying to get my head around the weird experience we had gone through. For the record I hardly slept a wink all night. I just hope Beth had a better night than I did. I remember dozing off countless times, only to be woken by this sharp stabbing pain in my back accompanied by a tugging sensation. I must have lain there for hours waiting to hear mom's alarm go off. Mom usually sets the alarm for 6:30.

I got up very achy and tired, got washed, cleaned my teeth, dressed and went downstairs. I went to mom in the kitchen. She was just making a cup of tea. "Morning, Oliver," mom said, "You look really tired. I heard you tossing and turning in the night. Is there something worrying you? Don't you feel very well?" I said, "Mom, stop fussing, I'm ok." Mom said Look, Oliver, if you are not feeling very well it does not matter about taking the money to Mrs Devere this morning. I can take it sometime next week " "No, mom, I've told you I am ok. It's just that for the past two nights I've had these pains in my back and this strange tugging sensation in my spine." Mom said, "lift your shirt up and let me have a look at your back." I did as mom said.

I could feel mom gently pressing different parts of my spine. Mom said, "Oliver, did it hurt anywhere when I was pressing on your spine?" I replied, that's the strangest thing mom it didn't, It hasn't been hurting in the day but I do get this occasional tugging feeling in my back." "Well, Oliver, my dear, you have got a bit of a knobbly spine anyway. I'm afraid you take after your father for that. His back was just the same. But I did notice that down towards the lower part of your back, your skin looked a bit red. In the same area three or four of your vertebrae are slightly more prominent than the rest. If you are not better by Monday I will book an appointment for you to see the doctor. You might have strained or pulled your back, Oliver. So, see how you feel over the weekend." "Thanks mom." Mom looked at me and said, "Fancy a bacon sandwich?" I said, "Mom, do I?"

Next to chips, that is one of my most favourite of all foods. With the smell of the bacon cooking, I was feeling better already. After my sandwich and a cup of sweet tea, I felt less tired. I asked mom for the money for Mrs Devere, she gave it to me in an envelope with Mrs Devere's name written on it. I suppose in case I lost it and hoped some honest person would hand it in. Oh yeah, and pigs will fly. I shouted to mom on my way through the front door, "I'm going now, mom. Isn't it a bit too early, Oliver?" mom replied. I shouted back, "I am going round to Mill', I mean Ruebens." Mom likes me to call him by his proper name. Mom shouted, "Ok then, see you later."

As I walked down the path, I tried listening for my favourite squeaky gate but no such luck. Oh well, I will be seeing her this afternoon. I made my way round to Milly's. Just before I got there I could have sworn I heard a tapping noise. Only two or three taps. It was in the distance, but it still sent shivers down my spine. I looked around, but like before there was nothing. I ran the rest of the way to Milly's. I thought at least there will be two of us. But my luck was out. Milly and Ruby had gone out for the day. I mean it's daylight and there are a few people around, I shouldn't be scared, should I? But I was. So much so that I waited for somebody to come along so I could walk with them or behind them. As luck had it, the first people to come along were Mr and Mrs Baldwin, who lived just across from us. An elderly couple but really nice and friendly, which is what I needed right now. We chatted about this and that as we walked into town.

I tried not to listen to anything that was going on behind me. Just a few furtive glances back every now and then. Still I saw nothing significant, just people going about their business, people coming to and from the town, dozens and dozens of people, to and froing. You would think that if somebody or something was following me, you would expect someone to have heard or seen something, but nobody has reported anything. Then it struck me, stopping me dead in my tracks, if there is only one of us, and it is following me, it is not following Milly, Ruby or Beth. Whatever it is, is after me and me alone.

"Oliver, are you alright? You are suddenly quiet and very pale. I had noticed how nervous you seemed to be when we met you. I noticed you kept looking behind you. Is somebody threatening you?" Mr Baldwin said with a concerned look on his face. "Is it that Jake Garnett again? We had heard about him assaulting you and about Mr O'Conner's house being broken into and being ransacked. All the people in the area know who is committing these crimes. Why isn't he in jail"? "Yes, Mr Baldwin, that is something that completely baffles me. The police say that nobody ever sees him committing these crimes. They never find any evidence or fingerprints. They've even searched his home. Still nothing. Anyway, Mr and Mrs Baldwin, do not worry. There will come a day when they will slip up."

I thought I had forgotten mom's letter she had asked me to deliver. Panic I thought I had lost the envelope. I pulled it out of my inside pocket. It had me in a panic for a moment there. We had now reached the high street and the Baldwins had told me they were going to the supermarket, which meant they would have to turn right on the high street. My destination was straight on. Boy what a life changing destination that turned out to be!

I thanked the Baldwins for letting me walk with them and for their company. Mr Baldwin narrowed his eyes and gave me a knowing smile. I believe he is quite a shrewd man, I don't think for a minute I had fooled him. He knew something quite serious was worrying me. But before we parted company, I asked the Baldwins if they had heard how Mr O'Conner was. I told her I had asked Mrs Addison about a week ago at school how her father was. She had said he was not very good and does not recognise anybody now. slip up.

I thought Mrs Baldwin said, "Oliver, don't be upset as tears welled up in my eyes he is in hospital now, he is in good hands." I tried to fight back the tears, but I lost. The tears started running down my cheeks. Mrs Baldwin put her hand on my arm and said, "I am so sorry, dear. I know he means a lot to you." She drew a couple of tissues out of her handbag and gave them to me, and said, "Here, dear, wipe your eyes." Which I quickly did.

If anybody sees me crying here I'll lose my street cred. You know, macho thing and all that and it's not as if I had any street cred anyway. One of these days I will find out what the hell it means. While wiping my eyes I could smell this nice perfume on the tissues. Without thinking, I went to give the tissues back to her. She put her hand up and said, "No dear, I think you had better keep them." Good job she did say, 'keep them' as I had blown my nose on one of them. I thanked the Baldwins once more and they carried on their way. Almost in unison, they said, "Take care and we will see you soon." I thought, thank god we have people like that in the world, kind and thoughtful.

I started to make my way to Mrs Devere's, lost in thought about poor Mr O'Conner, head down. I noticed somebody was blocking my way. I instinctively tried to step to my right, saying 'sorry' but this person put his arm out to stop me. Then this very slurred voice said, "It's me, Oliver me boy." As soon as I heard his voice, I instantly knew who it was. It was the town drunk, but a nice town drunk, who happens to be a lord, Lord Ponsonby Smythe. Everybody in the town loved him. You see the townspeople knew why he drank, and most days seeing him drunk in the town was never an issue for them. He always went drinking in the Pig and Whistle at the top of the high street. I have often seen him in the town. He tends to lurch about a bit, but I have never seen him fall over.

The life of Lord Ponsonby Smythe is not a very smooth one. He lives in a huge castle surrounded by a moat. He owns large tracts of farmland which he rents out, so I've been told. They also say he owns a lot of properties in the area including some businesses as well employing over five hundred townspeople. He is a kind, big hearted man who gives huge amounts of money to charity. He even paid for the new surgery to be built, including all up-to-date equipment. All this was of great annoyance to his shrew of a wife. This was his second wife, his first wife died a few years ago. I had been told she was a real lady, a good wife to him and a wonderful mother to his only daughter.

People who had met his second wife say that she appeared to be a nice, pleasant woman before they married. But it seemed once she got her hooks into him she changed completely, spending money as if there was no tomorrow. The daughter absolutely hated her. She quite openly says that her dad's new wife only married him for his money. His daughter also said her dad hardly ever drank, if at all. He only started drinking a few months after being married to the witch as she called her. His daughter regularly comes to pick him up. I think the pub phones to tell her he is on his way. People who have seen her sometimes struggling to get him into the car have kindly gone and helped her. She profusely apologises for the drunken state of her father. People tell her of the great love and respect they have for her father and the only worry they have is for his health and well-being.

Most times when she comes to collect him, watching him singing to himself and lurching from side to side, is just too much for her and she bursts into tears. People who have seen her in such distress have often tried to console her. They say she repeats the words, 'I want my dad back, how he used to be, not like he is now. Everything was fine until that witch came into our family. And now this lovely, jovial, drunken person is standing in front of me. He has been talking to me for the past 10 minutes and except for the occasional word, here and there, I haven't a clue what he is talking about.'

But one thing you need to know about Lord Ponsonby Smythe. He loves his takeaway meals, especially curries, and when I met him, he always asked me the same question. Any minute now he is going to give me some rather crude but I suppose essential advice. I know he would be alarmed when sober, at his behaviour in public. You know, being a lord of the realm, the things he says and does creates no offence to anybody. People in town noticed he had started drinking more heavily around March time, a few months after he had got married.

Although he is a lord and lives in a magnificent castle and was very rich he was regularly seen around the town, usually spoiling his daughter in the local shops. His daughter would always drop him off at the Pig and Whistle every Friday. He would have a drink and a good old knees up with the locals. Perhaps secretly, he would have liked to be just an ordinary person. He seemed to crave company and just loved chatting to people. Perhaps he felt lost rattling around in that big castle of his with his daughter and wife and a few servants for company. Anyway, he is still talking and I hate to be rude to him, so I said, "Sir, I'm sorry to interrupt you, but I have somewhere to go." "Oh, I am shorry, me boy." "That's ok, sir," I replied. Then he put his hands on my shoulders. I thought, oh no, he is going to give me his usual advice on constipation. I must have a constipated look about me because he always tells me the same thing every time.

God bless him. Hands on my shoulders, looking into my face and me looking into those pale blue blurry eyes. He had this great big mop of red hair and a big droopy ginger moustache. He had his red hunting jacket on, his big black riding boots. His pot belly was partially held in by his silvery patterned waistcoat with a gold chain draped across from one side to the other of his belly. One end of the chain disappeared into a little pocket in his waist coat which obviously held his fob watch. He gently swayed from side to side and combined with a strong smell of whiskey on his breath, it made me feel a bit dizzy.

Anyway, he continued to bestow this advice to me. "Oliver, my boy, how's your bowl?" "You mean my bowel, sir?" "It's ok. Thank you." "Look, Oliver, it is Oliver ishn't it?" "Yes, sir, it is." "If you ever get conshtipated, pop over to Mr Wongsh

Curry house, me boy. Worksh a treat. Guaranteed to pebble dash your toilet panch.." Swaying even more he said, "Did I just say panch?" And with a chuckle that rocked his rather generous pot belly said what I meant to shay Oliver wash panch." I said, "Thank you for the advice, my lord." He took his hands off my shoulders and walked away, saying with a side glance, "Oliver, my boy, my name is Rupert. Jush call me Rupert." I said, "Ok, thank you, Lord Rupert." That brought loud guffaws of laughter from him, ambling down the street, clapping his hands and laughing, he shouted, "Good one, Oliver, good one." With that, he disappeared into the crowds. What a character!

Mom was telling me a couple of weeks ago that she had heard how Lord Ponsonby Smythe had got himself into a bit of bother. Someone had told her that his daughter had picked him up from town one Friday. She told the police that her father appeared to be more drunk than usual. It took three people, including herself, to get him into the car. She said she had driven him home and with the help of the servants managed to get him out of the car. They eventually got him into the castle kitchen where she made him some strong coffee, which he drank two or three cups. He seemed to sober up a bit.

She said she had a very important appointment to go to, and left her father in the usual capable hands of the servants. It was only when she had a phone call from the police that she knew her father was in trouble. She later learned from the servants and the police what he had been up to. The servants told her that he kept talking about how he had forgotten his takeaway meal. The servants had offered to cook him a meal, but he was having none of it. He told them he was going to fetch his own meal. They told him he couldn't drive because he had been drinking. That didn't stop him.

He told his servant to saddle his favourite horse. The servant had no choice but to do as he was told. After several failed attempts to mount the horse he asked the very worried servant to bring his Range Rover alongside his horse, eventually climbing onto its bonnet, then onto his horse. He set off at a gallop towards the town. It's a miracle he managed to stay on the horse. The townspeople said they just watched in amazement as he came galloping down the high street on his beautiful white horse. Cars were swerving trying to avoid him until one car driver did not see him, and at the last moment slamming his brakes and, came to a screeching halt. Unfortunately the horse seeing the car in front decided to do the same.

That was not so good for Lord Ponsonby Smythe, doing a somersault over the top of the horse's head. They said he had landed on his back on the roof of the car. But the momentum made him slide across the roof down the rear window onto the car boot and then sliding off before disappearing behind the car. People feared the worst but they need not have worried because when they got to him they found him sitting on the road with his back against the bumper of the car happily unscrewing the cap off his silver whisky flask before taking a swig.

He said to the crowds surrounding him, "Cheers, cheers everybody." The crowd responded with a loud cheer for Lord Ponsonby Smythe. He replied, "No, no just call me Rupert." Everybody started to laugh. Then the crowd shouted, "Cheers, lord Rupert." Mom said she was told that brought him to tears. The doctor was fetched and on examining him, they couldn't find any injury, not even a scratch. After the police arrived and with protests from the crowd he was arrested and spent the night in the cells.

Lord Ponsonby Smythe was released the following morning into the arms of his tearful daughter. She looked into his face and said, "Dad, whatever possessed you to do such a thing? You could have been killed, dad, what have they charged you with?" He replied, "This will make you laugh. The police have charged me with riding a horse. under the influence…in other words, drunk in charge of a horse. They also charged me with causing damage to property. I presume they mean the car. But the driver of the car, god bless his soul, refused to press charges. Still under the influence, still blurry eyed, he said, I had dented the roof, and boot lid of the poor man's car. What a fright he must have had when he saw me bearing down on him on my big white charger."

Mom said the lord offered to buy him a new car but the man refused. Mom said he may be charged with endangerment to life as his actions were quite reckless. He had put an advert in the local newspaper apologising to all the people in the town of Wychwood for his behaviour. There was a photograph in the same newspaper where he had advertised Lord Ponsonby Smythe's daughter Charlotte, stating that her father was so ashamed of himself especially after being arrested he had now given up drinking altogether.

Well almost ha ha. Also, on the evening of her father's horse riding incident she had a meeting out of the town with a private detective she had hired to investigate her stepmother. The detective had told her that her stepmother was wanted by the police for embezzlement and fraud in London. But the best part was when the detective had told her that he had found out that her stepmother was already married to a Mr. Tomkins, Charlotte had said she was absolutely elated by the news. Because it meant she had committed bigamy. And, of course, had no hold over her father. Charlotte had stated she was very happy now that she had her father back and that her stepmother had been arrested and was awaiting trial. She had also said that she believed her so-called stepmother was the reason her father had taken to drinking. What a guy!

With my head down, I continued up the street hoping nobody would notice my red eyes. The news about Mr O'Conner really got to me. Although generations apart, I think of him as a close friend. I owe him a debt of gratitude for doing what he did for me, saving me from Jake the snake. Because now the more I think about it, the look in Jake's eyes just before he hit me, was of pure hatred. I really believe that if Mr O'Conner had not intervened when he did, Jake would have finished the job, I mean kill me. I don't think Jake particularly likes anybody, but why he has this intense hatred for me is a complete mystery. I thought at least Mr O'Conner has had a few months with his daughter. All those years wasted are really sad. Anyway, I carried on walking up the high street. Thinking about the story mom had told me.

I stopped and was looking in this shop window. It was a shop that sold ornaments and knickknacks. That was actually the name of the shop, yes, 'Knickknacks'. I was looking for something nice for mom as it is her birthday next week. There were quite a few ornaments that I think mom would like. So I decided that after I had been to Mrs Devere's, I would pop back later and have another look at the ornaments. I was about to move when I sensed that somebody was standing directly behind me. My skin prickled and I felt the hairs stand up on the back of my neck.

I instinctively looked at the reflection in the shop window to see who it was behind me. I had this strange foreboding that was not good and there sure enough was the evil grinning face of Jake the snake, as Milly likes to call him. I turned to face him. He looked bigger than ever. He has always been a bit taller than me, but now he seemed to tower over me. I realised that his brother Gary was with him, just standing there glaring at me. I looked around to see if anybody would help me. But everybody was giving us a wide berth. They just looked.

People passed by because they did not want to get involved. They were just too scared. They knew what the Garnett family were capable of doing to them and their family. But I was really scared. I am in the middle of the town on the main high street that is bustling with shoppers and I have nobody to help me, not even Milly. Not even the police, although I seem to remember there were always at least two policemen that patrolled the high street on a Saturday, which gave me a glimmer of hope. I was so absorbed looking for help I didn't hear what Jake was saying to me, it was only when I heard Beth's name mentioned, his foul mouth had mentioned my girlfriend's name, that brought me back to earth with a bump.

Now I was not scared but very angry. I looked into those cruel, evil eyes and gritted my teeth in sheer anger. I said, "What did you say?" With the palm of his hand, he struck me in the middle of my chest knocking me back into the plate glass window of the shop. I felt the glass shudder as my back and head struck it. I heard a man's voice from inside the shop shout, "What the hell is going on out there?" He briefly poked his head out of the shop doorway, saw Jake and quickly disappeared back into the shop.

Jake had now grabbed me by my coat lapels, virtually lifting me off the floor. He was talking to me. I could feel droplets of spit landing on my face. His breath smelled absolutely vile. As if a dying dog had crawled into that cavernous mouth of his and died in there. In every sense of the word, he made me feel sick. I knew he wasn't going to let me go this time. He said very slowly and very menacingly,

"You are going to take a walk with us because we have a date with your girlfriend. She is waiting for you down by the river and you and Beth are going to feed the fish, literally."

Now I had gone back to not being scared, I was now absolutely terrified. I thought, dear god, I can only hope he is lying about Beth. Gary started to laugh when he could see how scared I was. Jake snapped at him. "Shut your mouth, Gary." Which he promptly did, saying sorry, Jake, sorry" I took one last frantic look around to see if there was anybody that could help me. I saw what I had been looking for. I caught sight of the top of a policeman's helmet. First one, then the other, sunlight glinting off the badges on their helmets. Next to Beth, I've never seen a more beautiful sight. The trouble is they were on the other side of the high street and quite a way back.

Jake noticed me looking across the street. Still gripping me by my coat lapels turned his head to see what I was looking at. Jake spotted the police helmets amongst the crowds. His head snapped back round towards me. Grinning, he said, "Look, you little creep. You don't think these two coppers are going to help you, do ya? Nobody can help you anymore. Well, we can rule out that stupid Irish O'Conner, can't we? Not even that weird Devere woman you were going to see. I thought to myself, how the hell does he know that? Jake stopped grinning and looked straight into my eyes.

I stared back into those soulless eyes of his and I knew I was looking into the depths of hell. Then Jake said something rather strange. "You don't even know what a strange weirdo you really are, do you?" He released one of my lapels. His voice took on an angry tone through gritted teeth. Pointing to the ground he said, "You should not be here." Then pointing to the sky, he said, "That is where you should be, up there with that creep of a father of yours.

Now I could really feel unstoppable anger burning inside of me. What is he saying? That my father is dead? It goes without saying that Jake intends for me to join my father sooner rather than later. The thought that I would never meet my father is bad enough, but the thought these two thugs were going to harm my Beth became unbearable. The pent-up anger in me just exploded. I bought my two clenched fists up in front of me and drove them into Jake's chest as hard as I could, taking both of them completely by surprise. Jake staggered back with a look of complete disbelief on his face. I could not believe what I had just done. Jake and his brother Gary just stood there.

For the first time I saw fear in Jake's eyes. The look of fear did not last long as in the next few seconds, his face took on a grimace of sheer anger. He spat out the words, "You little creep, you and your girlfriend are going to pay for that." His fists clenched, he started to move towards me. All of a sudden I felt that familiar tugging sensation, but this time the pulling was in my chest and not my back. Jake stopped dead in his tracks. He seemed to sense that something was happening to me. I know that he had started to back away from me.

That look of fear had returned to his eyes. Does Jake know something I don't? Jake and Gary seemed really nervous. They were looking around everywhere, scanning up and down the high street. Who are they looking for? Maybe the policeman? Then I thought no, because where Jake and his family are concerned, the law does not seem to pose a threat at all. After they had finished looking around they seemed satisfied that whoever they had been looking for was not in the vicinity.

Jake now turned back to me and that sickly grin had returned. He started punching his right fist into the palm of his left hand. What happened next took us all by surprise.

Amazing, but very frightening at the same time. At first I felt quite a gentle tug in my chest. This was starting to unnerve me. My god, is this how a heart attack feels? But the next thing that happened eclipsed everything that had ever happened to me previously in my life. After the first gentle tug came a much sharper tugging, making me stumble forward.

It was the next pull that was so very frightening. This pull was so powerful that it virtually lifted me off my feet. I uncontrollably leaped forward, my legs pumping like crazy, trying to stop myself from falling on my face. I saw Jake frantically trying to get out of my way, as the next pull shot me forward like a rocket. Luckily, he was off balance when my shoulder struck his shoulder. I felt a stabbing pain in my shoulder from the collision but the pain was worth it because out of the corner of my eye I saw Jake crash into Gary, sending them both sprawling into the gutter, just where they belong.

The momentum continued. It was like being pulled by a rope attached to my chest. It had pulled me into the roadway. All of a sudden, the pulling stopped. I was suddenly aware of this white van coming towards me, to my right. The driver was honking his horn for me to get out of the way which I promptly did. Immediately after the van had passed me, there was this almighty bang. The van just stopped dead, its front completely caved in its rear end had lifted about three feet off the ground on impact. Whatever the van had run into must be very heavy and solid perhaps a lorry coming the other way.

Crowds started to appear around the front of the van. Some people were helping the driver get out of the van. I looked behind me and saw Jake and Gary getting to their feet. I quickly made my way to the front of the van. This could be my chance to get away from Jake and co. I pushed my way through the crowds squeezing myself through the throngs of people surrounding the van. I eventually managed to get to the inner circle of the people and looking over the top of this quite small woman's head.

I could see two policemen, probably the ones whose helmets I had spotted earlier. One had taken his helmet off and was scratching his head, looking really puzzled. The other policeman was busy trying to hold the crowds back. I could just see the van driver. He was sitting on the floor with his back against the van's front bumper, that is, what was left of it. The passenger side of the van was completely caved in. It was crushed so badly that had anybody been in the passenger seat they would have almost surely been killed.

I could hear the van driver moaning in pain. I heard somebody say they think he might have broken both of his wrists. They were saying the impact was so severe that he was thrown forward with so much force that he may have some internal injuries as well. They reckon the seat belt might have saved his life. The policeman who had been scratching his head now got down and spoke to the driver. He said to him, "Don't worry, son, the ambulance will be here any minute now. What's your name, son?" The driver replied with a struggle and with his eyes closed and obviously in a lot of pain, "Da … David." "Ok, David, I have just got to ask you this. What did you run into?"

The driver just shook his head from side to side. Then I heard a man's voice from the crowd shouting, "I'll tell you what? The van hit absolutely nothing. I saw the van coming down the street and there was this loud bang and the van just stopped dead. There was nothing at all in front of him." The policeman said, "Are you sure there were no cars or traffic of any sort?" The man replied, "No, definitely not." Dozens of other people spoke up and all said the same thing. Well, just another mystery in the town of Wychwood.

My main priority is to get to a phone box to ring Beth to see whether hopefully she is safe and at home. I remembered there's a phone box about a hundred yards up the high street. The problem, it is on the same side of the street where I had just left Jake and Gary. I decided I would take a chance and go back to the same side of the street I was originally on. That way I could see where the two evils were. I now made my way to the outer edge of the crowds, trying to make sure they hadn't come over and mingled in with the crowds.

So far, so good. It was only when I reached the last few people there was a slight gap and that is when I spotted them. To my relief they were walking away back down the high street. They were going in the direction that I had first come from. I waited with bated breath to make sure they were far enough away before I made my break. I waited for them to reach the corner.

As they reached the corner, Jake suddenly stopped and turned around and looked directly at where I was standing. There was no grin this time. With his lips curled back from his teeth it was more of a snarl than anything. He turned and pointed straight at me and did the same gesture as he did in the hospital corridor, running his thumb across his throat. He then turned, and both disappeared around the corner. I had to get to the phone box. I squeezed past the last few people in the crowd. There were lots of people on the pavement. It would only slow me down so I ran on the roadway, dodging the traffic as best I could.

I could see the phone box, but I could also see someone was in it using the phone. There was a very large lady using the phone. She wore this hat with a large feather in it, gold rimmed glasses and a very stern look on her face. At times it looked as if in between talking, she seemed to be chewing something, a wasp maybe? God help the wasp. I stood there waiting. God, I wonder how long she was going to be. I looked at the woman again, hoping she would realise that I was waiting to use the phone. She still had this angry look on her face. Perhaps it was that ill-fitting suit she was wearing which looked about five sizes too small for her. She looked as if she was ready to explode any second.

I was wishing that she would so I could use the phone. I was getting really worried now about Beth, so I walked up to the phone box and shouted through the glass to the woman, "I need to use the phone. It is an emergency." The woman went red in the face and very angrily pointed to the phone, mouthpiece and said, "And so is this." Then turned her back on me. I was now starting to panic. I did suspect that Jake may have been lying about Beth, but I could not take that chance.

Then a miracle, the woman had finished talking and just put the phone down. I made a dash to the phone box door just as the woman was coming out. She gave me a withering look and walked off. I got into the phone box as quickly as I could, fishing out my little notebook. It was a little leather-bound notebook that mom had bought me. I kept all my phone numbers in it, including Beth's which I was feverishly looking for. I found it, put my money in, dialled the number, pressed a button and waited for someone to answer and after a few seconds Beth's mother answered the phone.

I pressed the button and spoke to her, "Hello, Mrs Granger, can I speak to Beth please?" She replied, "Oh, hello Oliver. Of course, I'll just call her." I heard her shout, "Beth, it's Oliver for you." Then I heard Beth's sweet voice reply. "Ok, mom." She came to the phone and said 'hello'. I said to Beth, "Thank god you're alright." She replied, "Er, Oliver, why shouldn't I be alright?" and sounding very concerned, "Oliver, what has happened?"

I set about trying to explain to her what Jake had told me. "He had more or less kidnapped you. That you were tied up, somewhere down by the river, and if I didn't go with them they threatened to throw you in the river." "Well, they didn't and I am ok," Beth said. "There has to be something we can do about that family. Beth, the mother, is a really nice woman, a good soul. Why she tolerates that scumbag of a husband I will never know. It's the men of the family that are the problem. Sorry Beth, but I have to go. I still have to find your aunt, Mrs Devere, but I will see you this afternoon. Love you Beth. Bye." "Love you too Oliver. See you later."

I put the phone down and scanned up and down the high street through the glass side panels of the phone box. I had to be sure because it would be just like them to sneak back. Jake is not the sort of person who would give up easily. I cautiously opened the phone box door, looked around. Thankfully, no sign of them. I made my way to Mrs Devere's shop. I looked into Mrs Devere's shop window. I noticed an assortment of polished stones and large and small pieces of crystal lying on what looked like a deep red velvet cloth.

There were numerous figurines of American Red Indians. Then I noticed a large white sign with black lettering. Hanging on chains from the ceiling towards the back of the window display, it read [Mrs Alexis Devere, international psychic medium]. Private readings inquire within. I checked my coat pocket to make sure I still had the money It was still there. I thought, right, I had better go in. I put my hand on this very ornate shop door handle and as I grabbed it and before I had a chance to turn it, I had this strange overpowering sensation. I just froze on the spot, unable to move.

Then, just like in a movie I started to get flashbacks. The first flashback was the nightmare I used to get quite frequently until a few months ago. The flashbacks seemed to be running at quite a speed – waterfall, man on the hill, little China man, creature, cave, telephone, me falling off the cliff. Then it jumped to the frightening face of Jake, Jake's fist coming towards me, blackness, Mr. O'Conner's kindly face, mom, Mrs Addison, Jack, Milly, Ruby, Beth.

A brief flashback to when we were running to the pictures. That was when I first had that tugging sensation in my back. It jumped to today with Jake pushing me into the shop window, then me leaping forward as if somebody was pulling me by my chest with a rope, the van colliding with something, all of a sudden it stopped. I found myself being able to move again.

Am I having a mental breakdown? Hallucinations, what is happening to me? I turned the handle and entered the shop . It was just like mom had said, there was a wooden carved head of an American Indian, shelves full of crystals and polished stones, more Red Indian figurines. The things I think that look like tennis racquets with feathers are called dream catchers. I wonder if they have a nightmare catcher. I personally could have done with one.

There was a strong scent in the air. I seemed to recognise the smell. It was quite a pungent odour. I believe it's one of those scented sticks that they burn. Mom sometimes lights one if she has been cooking fish or cooking something with garlic in it. I prefer the smell of fish or garlic. But mom knows best. Mom had told me that when I go into the shop I will see a beaded door curtain directly in front of me, and I should just quietly shout to Mrs Devere to let her know I am there. Just in case, she might have a client in there with her.

But before I could do anything a woman's voice from the other side of the door curtain shouted, "Hello, who's there?" The sudden shout made me jump. Already nervous? That might make it a bit more so. I replied in a bit of a shaky voice.

"It's just me, Oliver, Mrs Devere, Alice's son." She replied, "Oh yes, Oliver, come on through." I approached the door curtain. I heard her say, "Stubborn woman. Told her not to bother about the money." I put my hands together as if in a prayer and speared my way through the bead curtain. Which rattled like hell.

As I entered the room the first thing I saw was the top of Mrs Devere's head. I noticed her hair was a similar blonde as Beth's. She was sitting at this small round table covered in what looked like a lace tablecloth with tassels around the edges. There was a large crystal ball in the centre of the table. She seemed to be intently studying what I recognised to be tarot cards. The only reason I know what they are is mom has a pack as well. She was so engrossed in what she was doing she didn't even bother looking up at who entered the room.

Arm outstretched towards me wagging her hand as if petting a dog, she said, I'm so sorry about this, Oliver, you will have to excuse me, but a very good friend of mine is quite ill at the moment. She can't come in and see me." She suddenly paused and turned a card over, and said "Oh dear," and wrote something down on a notepad. I noticed she was left-handed, the same as Beth. "Sorry, Oliver, as I was saying, my friend asked me to do a tarot reading for her. It's a bit odd doing a tarot reading like this when she is not here," She continued to turn the cards, writing the results on her notepad. She suddenly said, you know, I send out absent healing all the time, so what if I do an absent tarot reading? What is the difference? She chuckled at that. "You see I promised to phone the results to her later. Nearly finished, Oliver." It's ok, Mrs Devere At no time did she even look up once. I could've been Jack the Ripper for all she would know.

All of a sudden I heard the swish of the beaded curtain. It was swinging about wildly. I thought somebody's come into the shop and a gust of wind had come through. Without saying anything to Mrs Devere I went to investigate. I looked all around the shop, but there wasn't anybody there so I returned to the back room and waited for Mrs Devere to finish.

In the meantime I had a look around this wonderful room. One thing about it, it certainly had an atmosphere. The ceiling was the thing that took my breath away. The whole of the ceiling was covered in this dark blue colour, a myriad of silver reflective stars and in the centre of the ceiling was a bell-shaped chandelier, somewhere hidden in the glittering crystals of this odd shaped chandelier there must have been a small bright light.

Something that I had not noticed until now was that the chandelier was turning very slowly, probably powered by a small electric motor. This made the stars twinkle as the light from the chandelier struck the reflective surface of the stars. Mom never told me about this. Absolute magic. There was only one window in the room. The white blinds were shut and seemed out of character with the rest of the room. She had heavy red curtains, each side of the window held back with gold tassel tiebacks. There was this beautiful deep red chaise longue behind the back of Mrs Devere, and towards the far corner of the room.

There was this expensive looking carved table. On top of the table was a white centre runner table cloth, the ends coming to a point and had gold tassels. On this centre cloth was an array of objects. The first two objects were ceramic ceramic hands, one bigger than the other, possibly male and female. I could just make out lines on the palm of the hands, obviously for palm reading. Next to the hands was this shiny ceramic head. On the top I could see lines drawn and what happened to be small writing over the top of its head, I could just make out the word phrenology written on its very small ceramic chest.

There were glass balls of different sizes, some seemed to have something set inside the glass globes. One in particular caught my attention. It appeared to be three witches sitting around a cauldron It looked as if it was made of a heavy grey metal. The witches and a cauldron supported a large glass globe. Definitely a woman's room. On three of the walls were these patterned glass wall lights, giving off a soft yellow glow. A dark red short pile carpet covered the floor of this incredible room. The colours, globes and tassels everywhere? Definitely not a trace of male influence here. The only masculine thing in the room was that silly pottery head over there. All I could think was, wow. In this room, I wouldn't know whether to dance or go to sleep. I think I could do both here.

I watched Mrs Devere as she carefully packed away her tarot cards. As she was closing her notepad and still with her head inclined forward, looking at me through a corner of her eye while she continued to tidy her table, she said something that surprised me, "By the way Oliver, have you brought somebody with you?" I replied, "No, Mrs Devere, I'm on my own." "Oh, I am sorry, Oliver, I thought I felt or sensed somebody was with you. My mistake." "That's ok, Mrs Devere." She patted her notebook and the pack of tarot cards and said, "Right, all neat and tidy now. Oliver, what can I do for you?"

And for the first time since I had entered the room, she was looking directly at me. But not for long. Her eyes left mine, and with only a slight movement of her head.

In those last few seconds she had looked at me I saw a striking resemblance to Beth, especially those big green eyes that were now darting towards the upper corner of the room directly behind me. Her eyes were getting bigger by the second. Her jaw dropped, mouth wide open and with a look of sheer terror on her face, whatever she thought she was looking at had frightened her so much, making her stand up with such ferocity it sent her chair flying backwards, striking the wall behind her with a dull thud.

She continued her backward motion towards the opposite corner of the room. She collided with the table, making the ornaments clink together. She continued to stare wild eyed into the corner, obviously terrified. I looked into the corner she was looking at to try and find what had frightened her so much.

I could see nothing, not even a spider which I have to admit, can be quite frightening. I turned back to Mrs Devere. She was now clutching the tassel of the centre table cloth. She let out this ear piercing scream, at the same time pulling the tassel up to her mouth as if to stifle her scream. Which then sent most of the ornaments crashing to the ground. Three of the fingers on the larger hand snapped off, the glass orbs bounced and clattered together, one managed to bounce and roll, finally coming to rest with a bump against the skirting on the opposite side of the room.

I attempted to walk towards Mrs Devere to try and comfort her. I had only taken a couple of steps when Mrs Devere shouted at me, "Oliver, please stay where you are." I said "Mrs Devere, please tell me what you have seen? Is it a ghost or lots of ghosts? Mrs Devere, with the greatest of respect, don't you talk to dead people or ghosts? I thought you would be the last person to be frightened of a ghost." The next words she spoke were with a raised panic in her voice. "Oh my dear god. Oliver, what the hell have you brought in with you?"

End of volume one.......

This is my youngest son James Poetry.
Mary Bella makes her claim.
She once was the one to blame.

But now her path is clear.
For all the fortune she holds dear.

This is. Not who or what.
But pure magic is what she's got.

Now comes the time for her to
meet the all divine.
It's set in time and space.
But where is this place?
The all-knowing watching eye has its moment in the sky.
Do you see?
The door was in vain.
Look for the sun through the rain.
You will see Mary Bella's door.
Don't forget, even she was once poor.

So, there you have it.
The magic of Mary Bella.

And all she did was follow. Red, blue and yellow.
Now she has all she needs to know.

She just might have found the end of the rainbow.